LEGION OF THE DEAD

THE INVISIBLE DETECTIVE
LEGION OF THE DEAD

BY JUSTIN RICHARDS

SIMON AND SCHUSTER

Acknowledgements

As ever I am indebted to my family – Alison, Julian
and Christian – for their patience, comments
and love, and to my editor, Stephen Cole,
for his comments, patience and confidence.

SIMON AND SCHUSTER

First published in Great Britain by Simon & Schuster UK Ltd, 2005
A Viacom company

Copyright © Braxiatek Ltd, 2005
Cover illustration © David Frankland, 2005

The right of Justin Richards to be identified as author of this
work has been asserted in accordance with sections 77 and 78
of the Copyright, Designs and Patents Act, 1988.

1 3 5 7 9 10 8 6 4 2

Simon & Schuster UK Ltd
Africa House
64-78 Kingsway
London WC2B 6AH

A CIP catalogue record for this book is available from the British Library

ISBN 1 416 90106 X

Typeset by SX Composing DTP, Rayleigh, Essex
Printed and bound in Great Britain by Cox & Wyman, Reading, Berkshire

For Alison, Julian and Christian – as ever

CHAPTER ONE

The fog was so thick that Constable Jennings could barely see his own boots. He shone his torch into the gloom and shivered despite his heavy police cape. Who would have thought he would need it in the middle of summer? The air tasted of smoke and the river and it muffled any sounds. A cab might pass within ten feet of him and he would neither see nor hear it.

Cursing the unseasonably cold weather, Jennings stamped some feeling back into his feet and made his way carefully up the street. He had stepped off the pavement and into the gutter twice already. He almost went sprawling the first time, slipping on the greasy cobbles.

From nearby he fancied he heard a scraping like someone sharpening a blade on a whetstone. A metallic clang that must be a boat on the river. Instinctively, he turned towards the noise, shining his light at a wall of fog. The sounds must be loud for him to hear them so clearly through the heavy night. He listened for a moment more, but they were not repeated. So he shone the light at his watch instead and was pleased to see that he went

1

off duty in twenty minutes. Time to complete his rounds, and then home for a cup of tea and good night's sleep. After his usual pint of beer in the Dog and Goose, of course.

With a more optimistic spring in his step now, Jennings continued on his way. His mind was already on the warmth of his home and the end of his shift. Which was why he almost missed the dark shape that loomed up at him out of the fog.

It was a man. His pale face appeared in the light from Jennings's torch. Just for the briefest instant – caught startled. Then the man gave a surprised gasp, turned away and disappeared back into the fog. Jennings stared after him as the mist rolled back in and papered over where the man had been.

A clink, barely noticeable. Jennings almost missed that too. But somehow he knew the startled man had dropped something. Something small, metallic. His torch picked out the glimmer of the coin lying on the pavement. Jennings stooped and picked it up. It slipped under his fingers and he needed to put down the torch and pull off his glove to pick it up. Then he stuffed it into his pocket and shouted after the man.

The only reply was the muffled click of nailed boots on the pavement ahead of him. Jennings gave a sigh and hurried after the man. He fancied he could hear another sound now – the jangling of coins or keys in the man's pockets as he ran.

'You there – hold on!' Jennings shouted.

The fact that the man seemed determined not to stop spurred him on. What did the fellow have to hide? What had he been up to? After all, there was nothing here except the river and the graveyard. Jennings shivered at the thought.

Then he heard the cry. It was a shocked, frightened shout of distress from somewhere close by. Choked off. Jennings skidded to a halt, looking round as he tried to work out what it was and where it had come from. The torchlight barely scratched the surface of the fog. He grabbed his whistle and blew – piercing, shrill blasts that split the air like a sword.

In reply, he heard the slap of running feet off to his left. There was a side street – he could just make out the edges of the buildings that lined it. Jennings made his way cautiously along the narrow pavement, staring into the gloom for the slightest movement.

Even so, he almost stumbled over the body. His foot connected with the man and he had to struggle to keep his balance. He knelt down, sweeping his light over the prone form. In a moment he took in the fog-blurred shape of the man's coat, saw the lining of the pockets had been pulled out, tried not to dwell on the eyes staring up from the pallid face. He felt for a pulse, and was surprised to find one. But it was very faint, and getting fainter. Jennings swallowed hard, and blew his police whistle again.

Quickly, he patted down the man's clothes, searching for a clue and feeling for any wound. If it were not for the turned-out pockets, he might conclude that the man had slipped while running. The cobbles were slick and damp under the man's head, but it took Jennings a moment to work out why. Slipped and fallen and cracked his head open . . .

Maybe, after all, that *was* what had happened. For while some of the pockets were turned out, there was a hard, rectangular shape in the lining of one that, it transpired, was a silver snuff box. And the man's wallet was still in his hip pocket, untouched. What sort of thief would check the man's coat, but leave a silver snuff box and a wallet behind? An accident, then – a strange accident and a policeman's overactive imagination in the fog of the night.

Jennings blew out a long misty breath of relief and pulled himself to his feet. As he did so, his torch strayed and bobbed across the pavement. It shone briefly on the wall of one of the houses. And there, standing in the torchlight, was a figure.

The light reflected back off the armour the man was wearing. It picked out the leather chin strap under the polished helmet and the similar straps that held the sandals in place on the man's feet. It shone on the metal breastplate and the shoulder guards. Glinted on the short sword the man was holding, illuminating the cold stare of his flint-coloured eyes stabbing into the fog.

As Jennings gasped in surprise, the torch wavered, moving further along the wall, away from the man. And when Jennings immediately swung the torch back, there was no one there.

Confused, he swung the torch all round. But still there was nothing – just himself and the body at his feet. And, he realised as he thrust his hand into his pocket, the small coin he had picked up. He inspected it in the cold light of the torch. He had thought it was a sixpence as it was about the same size. But the edges were uneven and bent. It was discoloured and tarnished with age. The head that was on the coin was not that of the king, and not even that of the last king, or Queen Victoria. It was an arrogant profile of a man with a jutting nose.

It looked, Jennings thought, for all the world like a Roman emperor. Just as the man he had glimpsed in the torchlight – the man in armour, brandishing a short sword – had looked for all the world like a Roman soldier.

The darkened room was silent as Albert Norris finished his story. The curtains were drawn across the bay windows in the room above the locksmith's shop and the only light came from the lamp on a table at the back. In the gloom, the assembled people who had stood and listened to Norris's tale waited for the Invisible Detective to answer.

The detective himself – Brandon Lake – was seated in a high-backed armchair at the front of the room. The dilapidated chair faced away from his audience, so that the figure of the detective himself was all but hidden from view. There was the hint of a hat poking up, and the detective's hand emerged to punctuate his words with the occasional gesture as he spoke. His voice was deep and mellow, slightly throaty.

'A fascinating story,' the detective pronounced. 'An unidentified man who may have tripped or may have been pushed. And a mysterious figure who vanishes into the fog. Yes, fascinating. Tell me,' he went on, 'how do you come to know the facts, if indeed they are facts, in such detail?'

'Got 'em from the horse's mouth, didn't I?' Norris explained. 'Constable Jennings, he nips into the pub for a swift pint when he's finished on the beat.'

'I see. And he was unsettled enough by the events of the evening to share them with you and several of your patrons.'

'S'right, Mr Lake, sir.'

Norris was the landlord of the local pub – the Dog and Goose on Cannon Street. Several of his regular customers nodded and looked pleased with themselves. They had indeed heard the story straight from Jennings just a few evenings ago.

'Quite shaken up, he was,' Norris went on. 'Downed a pint of mild right off, then had another.' Norris laughed as he remembered. 'He always brings the exact money for his pint, he does. Reckon that's all his missus will let him have. You should have seen the look on his face when he realised he couldn't pay for the second pint.'

A couple of other men laughed with Norris as they too recalled the incident. 'Him a copper and all,' one of them added.

'A copper come a-cropper,' someone else muttered, provoking more laughter.

'That was why he told us what had happened,' Norris went on. 'Don't reckon he was supposed to say really, but we could all tell he needed his drink. The only thing he had left in his pocket after his first pint was this little coin. He slapped it on the bar and said it was all he had so could he stick the second pint on his tab and pay me tomorrow. I asked him what the funny little coin was and that's when he told us. Sort of blurted it out. Reckon it shook him up more than he'd admit.'

'So you allowed him the second pint on

account?' the Invisible Detective surmised.

But, for once, he was wrong.

'Well, I was so taken by his story that I thought it might be a case for you, Mr Lake.'

'Thank you.'

'So I took that strange little coin instead. Roman, Jennings said he thought it was. Well, I don't know about that. But it's got to be worth more than some of the dud coins getting passed around these days.'

'Dud coins?' the detective echoed.

'That's right. Forgeries and counterfeits. Had another florin that's no good the other day. But you'll know all about that, I'm sure. More than the rest of us, I expect. Anyway, I thought, that little coin may not be worth much, but at least I know what I'm getting. And a good story is always worth a pint.' Norris hesitated, realising what he had just said. 'A *good* story, mind. None of *your* tales, Josh Pinner. So,' he went on quickly as people chuckled at Josh Pinner's grunt of surprise, 'I popped that little coin in your tin when I came in, along with my sixpence. I reckon you'll make more of it than I could.'

Brandon Lake, the Invisible Detective,

sounded amused. 'Perhaps, Mr Norris. We shall see. And, if I do discover more about the coin and this strange story of Constable Jennings's, rest assured that I shall relay the information to you at one of our Monday evening sessions.'

Behind the dusty curtains that closed over the bay window stood three figures hidden from view. They listened attentively to Norris's story and to the detective's comments. One of them, a thin, dark-haired boy called Jonny, was holding a fishing rod. If any of them needed to get a message to the detective seated in the chair, then it was up to Jonny to flick the note across the darkened room and to pull back any reply.

Beside Jonny, Meg listened most carefully of all. Her face was set in a sullen, almost sulky expression, framed by a mass of curly auburn hair. She would know at once if anyone was lying. She had no idea how she did it, she could just tell. And if anyone did lie to the Invisible Detective, she would make sure that Jonny let him know.

Beside Meg, younger and smaller, was Flinch. Her blonde hair was stained almost brown, and her clothes were threadbare and old. She bounced excitedly on the balls of her feet as she listened to Norris's story. Her constant enthusiasm was one of the few things that could make Meg smile.

'Is the story true?' Flinch whispered to Meg.

Meg put her finger to her lips. The session was coming to an end and she waited for the sound of the people leaving – their feet thumping on the bare wooden stairs. Then she answered, still in a whisper, 'I don't know, Flinch. But Norris isn't lying. So that's what the policeman told him.'

'Art will know,' Jonny said quietly. He leaned the fishing rod in the corner of the window and then peeped through the narrow gap at the edge of the curtains. 'We can ask him in a minute.'

Once he could see that the room was empty, Jonny pulled back the curtains. He went at once to inspect the tin on the table next to the lamp – to count the sixpences people had paid to ask their questions.

Flinch and Meg waited behind the chair, as the Invisible Detective stood up and turned round. He was known as 'the Invisible Detective' because no one ever saw him. There was a good reason for this, and one that would have surprised Albert

Norris and his friends had they seen the figure now slipping off the large coat and removing the hat. Standing in front of Flinch and Meg was Art Drake.

Like Meg and Jonny, Art was just fourteen years old. Together with Flinch, the four of them made up the Cannoniers, named after Cannon Street, where the Invisible Detective held his consulting sessions, and also because the children used an old warehouse on Cannon Street as their den. Art flicked his brown hair back across his forehead and rubbed at his neck. His throat was slightly sore from putting on the deep voice.

'So, a mystery,' he said.

Flinch clapped with delight.

'An old coin and a spooked bobby,' Meg said. 'Not much of a mystery.'

'Don't spoil it,' Flinch said.

'No, don't spoil it,' Art said with mock severity.

Meg's mouth twitched, which for her was close to a smile. 'I won't spoil it,' she said. 'Maybe there is a mystery, but don't get your hopes up. It's probably nothing.'

'A foggy night and a man who slipped and

banged his head,' Art said, nodding. 'That is the most likely explanation, I have to agree.'

'But what about the Roman soldier he saw?' Flinch asked, sounding disappointed. 'And the coin.'

'He could have got the coin any time,' Jonny said as he joined them. He held the tiny piece of metal up for them to see. It was a rough circle, dark with dirt and tarnish. But the embossed face was still clear. 'Might be a keepsake the man dropped. Then Jennings got spooked. More of a mystery in tracing this counterfeit money Norris was on about.'

'Yes,' Art agreed. 'If he did actually pick up the coin before he thought he saw the Roman, then it might have planted the idea in his mind.'

'Just his imagination?' Flinch said. She looked down at her feet, her long hair falling forward so they could not see her crestfallen expression.

Meg put an arm round her friend's shoulders. 'That's only one explanation. We need to investigate to be sure.'

'Of course we do,' Art said. He took the coin from Jonny and inspected it carefully. 'And, if nothing else, we can have fun finding out more about this Roman coin. If it really is Roman.'

'How do we do that?' Flinch wondered.

'There's a little museum in Myton Gardens,' Jonny said. 'They've got Roman stuff. I go in there sometimes on the way home from school to get away from . . .' He broke off, his ears going slightly pink. 'Well, you know, just to have a look round. It's interesting. Anyway,' he went on quickly, 'there's a man there who runs the place, Mr Worthington. He'd know if it's really Roman.'

'Good thought,' Art said. 'The museum will be closed now, of course. So we'll have to go after school tomorrow.' He grinned and looked round at his friends, holding up the small coin for them to see. 'So, who's for a trip to the museum?'

The Myton Museum was a square Victorian building on the corner of Myton Gardens. From the outside, Art thought, it looked rather small. He and the other Cannoniers had spent time in the British Museum. Compared with that, the Myton Museum was tiny. It had an arched doorway with 1868 engraved on the keystone above. The doors were open, and Art could see Jonny standing under the arch, waiting.

It was no surprise that Jonny was here first. For one thing he had less distance to come. For another he was quick – Jonny could run faster than anyone else Art knew, child or adult. Jonny looked nervous, shuffling his feet impatiently and glancing out of the door frequently. He was looking the other way, so he didn't see Art for a while. When he did catch sight of his friend approaching, Jonny's face cracked into a grin.

'You all right?' Art asked.

'Yeah. Some of the boys from school, they follow me sometimes. I don't want them to know where I go.' He shrugged, as if it was nothing.

Art didn't press him to explain further. They all knew that Jonny had trouble with some of the older boys at his school, but he didn't like to talk about it. Jonny glanced again across the street before leading Art inside.

'Meg and Flinch not arrived yet?'

'Not yet,' Jonny confirmed. He was speaking quietly, despite the fact that the museum was empty.

Inside, the museum was a single large room.

A metal spiral staircase led up to a gallery above, where Art could see shelves full of books and papers. The downstairs was dotted with display tables and exhibits. The bones of a small dinosaur were wired together so that it stood – incomplete – at the bottom of the stairs. Three of the walls were lined with glass-fronted cabinets, inside which exhibits were arranged on shelves.

'The Roman stuff is over here.'

Jonny led the way across the museum towards the back wall. They passed a table with a model of London on it, as it had been before the Great Fire of 1666. Pieces of bone were arranged on another table, with flint arrowheads lined up beside them. A large lump of flat stone bore the imprint of an ancient clawed foot. One cabinet at the side of the room was full of stuffed animals – polecat, fox, badger, rat . . . The eyes stared glassily at Art and Jonny. Everything had a small cardboard label close by or attached – all written in the same neat copperplate hand.

The cabinet that filled the back wall was given over entirely to Roman relics and artefacts. There were fragments of mosaic, several statues washed almost shapeless by centuries of rain, a rusty sword with its blade broken, the metal point of a spear . . . And, in front of Jonny, a small pile of tiny silver coins. Their edges were ragged and bent, and the images on them worn almost flat. But the similarity to the coin that Art had in his pocket was startling.

'Where's the curator or whatever he is?' Art wondered.

'There's a little room out the back. I think he makes himself tea or something.'

Art turned, sensing movement behind him. It was Meg and Flinch. They were standing just inside the door, looking round with interest. Flinch saw Art and Jonny and ran over. Meg followed, taking her time, studying things she passed, just as Art had done.

'They're the same,' Flinch said, seeing the coins inside the cabinet. 'Oh, Jonny, you're so clever.'

Jonny beamed.

'I suppose they look a bit similar,' Meg conceded as she joined them.

Jonny was affronted. 'A bit?' Then he realised Meg was teasing and he grinned at her to show he knew.

There was a small door at the side of the large room, almost lost between the display cases and cabinets. Art had not noticed it until it opened and a small, dark-haired man emerged. His face was lined and saggy, though he looked only middle-aged, and his jacket was crumpled, as if he had slept in it. He saw the children at once and hurried over. He had, Art noticed as he approached, startlingly green eyes.

'Oh, my goodness me, visitors,' the man said. He sounded both flustered and excited in equal measure. 'I am sorry, I was in the storeroom.' He shook his head sadly. 'So much to catalogue and so little time in the day. What is the time?' he wondered, and checked a gold watch he pulled from his jacket pocket. 'Gracious,' he decided. 'Where does it go?' He stuffed the watch back into his pocket and clapped his hands together, his face breaking into a sudden smile. 'Now, then, are you just having a look round or can I help explain anything?' His eyebrows darted upwards hopefully. 'Anything at all?'

'Well, actually . . .' Art began.

But the man had spotted Jonny. 'It's young Mr Levin, isn't it? What a surprise. Yes, I certainly know you, young man. School work is it, again? Or just general curiosity?'

Jonny looked slightly embarrassed at this. He opened his mouth to answer, but Flinch beat him to it.

'We've got a coin,' she said. 'We think it's Roman.'

'Have you now? Well, that's very interesting. Perhaps I could take a quick look. Roman, eh?'

Art handed the man the coin. 'Are you Mr Worthington?' he asked.

The man nodded. 'Indeed, yes. Curator, historian and the Emperor Nero.'

'What?' Meg said, as startled as the others.

'Sorry. The coin here.' Worthington held it up for them to see. 'The image of the Emperor Nero. Unmistakable. Says so too, in Latin of course. Remarkably well preserved.' He peered at it closely again. 'Seems genuine. How extraordinary.'

'Why extraordinary?' Jonny asked.

'What? Oh, just because you'd expect it to be worn down rather more. Bit battered, used, knocked about.' Worthington pointed to the coins in the cabinet. 'Like those.'

19

'You don't think it's a counterfeit?' Art said.

'Oh, no no no no no.' His head was shaking violently. 'Who'd want to counterfeit an old coin? New ones, yes, there's reason enough for that.'

'So it's not worth anything?' Meg said.

'It is worth quite a lot actually, young lady. Though historically rather than financially. Mind you, if there were more of them . . .' He looked round at them all. 'Where did you say this was found?'

'We didn't,' Meg replied.

'I'm afraid we don't really know,' Art explained. 'It was given to us, but I don't know where it came from.'

'Such a shame, such a shame.' Worthington sucked air noisily through his teeth. But then he saw Flinch's disappointed expression and he smiled. 'After all,' he said, 'you never know. It could be part of the treasure of the Lost Londinium Legion.'

Flinch brightened at once. 'Treasure!'

He shrugged. 'You never know.'

Jonny and Art exchanged looks.

'What lost legion?' Jonny asked.

'Yes, I've never heard of it.'

'Oh, bit arcane, I'm afraid. Local legend, not much remembered now, I'm sure.' He was staring at the coin again. 'But the date fits. Let me see, Nero became emperor in, what, AD 54?' He turned to Art as if expecting to be corrected.

'If you say so,' Art said.

'I do,' Worthington decided. 'And the Lost Legion dates, if Tacitus is to be believed, to the period immediately before Boudicca was defeated by Suetonius Paulinus. So that would be AD 60 or 61. Near enough.'

'Boudicca was an ancient Briton, the queen of a tribe called the Iceni who led a rebellion against the Romans,' Art explained to Flinch. 'Hundreds of years ago. Nearly two thousand, in fact.'

'But what was this lost legion?' Meg was asking Worthington.

'No one really knows, I'm afraid. Just a vague mention in Tacitus of a group of highly experienced soldiers assembled for some sort of special mission to help defeat Queen Boudicca when she marched on London. Or Londinum as it was then. They were paid a vast fortune, so it's said.'

'And they got lost?' Flinch said.

'Well, they are never mentioned again, though Boudicca was indeed stopped and defeated about then. Tacitus mentions only a handful of men, perhaps a dozen. But that soon becomes a legion when stories spread. Hence the *Lost Legion*. Probably,' he confided in a quiet voice, 'it never existed in the first place.'

'But there is a treasure?' Flinch said, frowning.

Worthington smiled reassuringly. 'I'm sure there is. The fortune they were paid, probably in coins like this one, vanished with them.' He handed the coin back to Art. 'Now, if you discover where this was found, or if you happen across any more, I should be extremely interested. Thank you so much for letting me see it.'

Art smiled back, caught up in the little man's enthusiasm. He looked at the others. Meg gave the slightest of nods, realising what Art was thinking. He held the coin out again to Worthington.

'We'd like to donate this to the museum,' he said. 'If it's historically interesting, then you should have it.'

Worthington's mouth dropped open and his

eyes seemed suddenly moist. 'You are sure?' He reached out, hesitated, then carefully took the coin.

'You could put it in there,' Flinch said, pointing to the cabinet containing the other Roman coins. 'Then people can look at it.'

'I could indeed.' He nodded, excited at the thought. 'In fact, I shall. I must write a label at once. Tell me, who shall I put donated the coin? Mr Levin here?'

They all looked at Jonny. 'Say it's from Mr Brandon Lake,' Jonny said. 'He gave it to us.'

'Very well.'

'And the Cannoniers,' Flinch said. 'Cos it's from us too.'

It was sardines on toast for tea. Art wasn't that keen, but he was hungry. He ate them as quickly as he could, washing away the taste of the fish with a mug of sweet tea.

'Is there much trouble with counterfeiting at the moment?' he asked as he waited for Dad to finish.

'Who told you that?' Dad wondered.

'I don't know. Just heard it somewhere. Is it secret?'

Art's father was a detective sergeant at Scotland Yard and he would tell Art what he could. He wiped his mouth on his napkin and considered. 'There's more than we'd like. Coins, of course. But a few banknotes too. We've got people looking into it. Nothing to worry about yet.'

'Yet?'

'If someone's gone to the trouble of making the machinery to stamp out fake coins of the realm, they might as well produce thousands as a few dozen.'

'Maybe people aren't realising they're fakes,' Art suggested.

'They are very good ones,' Dad admitted. 'But no, my worry is that someone's just testing a few coins to see if they can get away with it. When they're happy they've got their mould right and the metal and weight and everything spot on, then they'll start to mass-produce them.'

'Which is a problem?' Art asked. 'I mean, I know it's against the law and everything, but it's not like robbery or murder, is it? No one gets hurt.'

Dad smiled and started to clear away. 'On the contrary, everyone gets hurt.'

'How's that?'

'If there is suddenly a lot more money going round, then it's not worth so much. People can't just make their own money without any wealth to back it, any more than the Bank of England could. How much things cost and what people get paid, they all depend on how much money there is to share out and cover costs, and that depends on how much the country earns by making goods and so on.'

'It all sounds rather complicated,' Art decided.

'Complicated and delicate. But if someone created enough fake money and dumped it into the system, our whole society could collapse. If suddenly there's enough money for us all to buy a car, then there won't be enough cars to go round. So the price of cars will go up until only the same number of people can afford a car as there are cars to be had.'

'I see,' Art said slowly. 'And I suppose that's true for everything, from aeroplanes down to bread and butter.'

Dad nodded. 'If everyone has more money, then everything costs more. You'll be paying a pound for a loaf of bread before you know it.'

'A pound?' Art whistled.

'Oh, and talking of money and coins,' Dad said, turning back from the sink, 'this might interest you.' He took something from his pocket, something small, and tossed it to Art. 'Know what that is?'

Art looked at it, nestling in the palm of his hand. He felt suddenly numb, his brain seemed to have stopped and he just stared. He could hear himself answering, 'It's a Roman coin, dating from the time of the Emperor Nero, who came to power in AD 54.'

Dad was looking at him in surprise. 'They do teach you something at school, then.' He laughed. 'It's Roman all right, and I'll take your word for it about Emperor Nero.'

'Dad, where did you get this?' Art asked. 'Was it in the Myton Museum?'

'The Myton . . .' Dad frowned, and sat down at the table next to Art. He took the coin back and examined it. 'No, though they probably do have

Roman coins there. No, I found it in a dead man's garden.'

The book was old. The pages were discoloured and brittle beneath Arthur Drake's fingers. The paper seemed even more yellow in the light from his bedside lamp. The casebook of the Invisible Detective – as kept by his grandfather, also called Arthur Drake. Art for short.

He had read and re-read it so many times. Sometimes he could remember what he had read, but at others it seemed to slip away like a dream when you wake up. Now he could remember it all.

All except the last few pages. The final case. The investigation that Art had called 'The Legion of the Dead'.

It was sad, Arthur thought as he closed the book. Sad that the adventures were coming to an end. The final case for the Invisible Detective back in London all those years ago. What had happened then, after the end of the book? Where had Art and Jonny and Meg and Flinch ended up? There was a war coming, though they did not know it. He thought they suspected, like so many people, but could not be sure. How had that changed them?

And they had grown up. Grown old. He had only to look at his own grandad to see that. It was so difficult to remember that Grandad *was* Art. So hard to reconcile the two people. Yet he knew it was true.

With a sigh, Arthur closed the book. He put it down on the bedside cabinet, turned out the light and snuggled under the covers. Just one more case, one more story. But not now. He would save it, enjoy it, make it last. If it was sometimes rather like a dream, then despite the fear and the excitement, it was one he wanted never to end.

Arthur Drake's eyes closed and he slipped into a peaceful sleep.

CHAPTER TWO

The Cannoniers met on the Wednesday afternoon at their den. It was an old, disused warehouse on the corner of Cannon Street. The afternoon light shone in through broken windows high in what had been the main storage and loading area. The windows that were still intact were so dusty that they let in hardly any light. They were just gun-metal squares above the rusty gantry that ran round the walls.

The last thing the warehouse had been used for, before it was abandoned and left to fend for itself against the elements and the stones thrown by local kids, was carpets. There were still many left – rolls of rotting, canvas-backed material haphazardly spread across the floor and propped up or stacked in precarious piles against the crumbling walls. As they decayed, they added to the dust that hung in the murky air.

In one corner, Flinch had made herself a soft bed out of some of the less decayed carpets. It was here that she spent her nights, curled up and warm, with only the occasional rat or mouse for company. But it was better than being out

29

on the streets. At least she had a roof over her head, even if it did leak. Though she wished she had her own, she did not envy the others their homes and families. She knew that Jonny was bullied at school and Meg was forever nervous at home. Flinch had a home all of her own and could share it with her own family – her best friends.

Now the four of them were sitting on rolls of carpet that were arranged like giant benches in the middle of the room. Flinch was perched cross-legged on top of one roll. She could smell the dust and age coming off it. Jonny and Art were sitting opposite, and Meg was on her own on a third roll of carpet.

'And then Dad said he found it in a dead man's garden,' Art was saying.

They all gasped.

'What dead man?' Flinch wanted to know. 'How did he die?'

Art smiled and held up his hand to stop their questions. 'Got me interested too, I can tell you. But it seems they identified the man Constable Jennings found, the man who dropped the coin we took to the museum.'

'If it wasn't just lying there in the street,' Meg said.

'I don't think it was,' Art told them. 'Because the police went to the man's house. His name was Derek Quainton, apparently. He was unconscious, but someone at the hospital recognised him. So the police traced his address and went to see if he had a wife or any family.'

'And did he?' Jonny asked.

Art shook his head. 'He lived alone and the place was quite run down, so Dad says.'

'Why did your dad go?' Meg wondered. 'He's a detective, not a foot plod.'

'They called for him because Quainton's house had been broken into. Ransacked.'

Flinch clapped her hands to her mouth. 'The poor man,' she said. 'He gets hurt and then he gets burgled.'

'Someone made sure he was out of the way,' Jonny said knowingly.

'It's likely,' Art agreed. 'Except, just as whoever attacked him didn't take that silver snuff box, Dad says that there didn't seem to be anything missing from the house.'

'How can he be sure?' Meg said. 'They don't

know what he owned. Or did they ask him to come and see?'

'They couldn't,' Art admitted sadly. 'He never came round from that bang on his head. The doctors say it's more likely he was hit with something than he fell. And he died from it.'

'So it's murder,' Jonny said grimly.

'Murder with no motive. He wasn't robbed. And his house was broken into but nothing was taken. There was some cash lying about – they found it but didn't take it. A couple of valuable paintings too, not to mention other bits and bobs.'

'What about the treasure coin?' Flinch wanted to know. 'Where was that?'

'Dad found it in the back garden, by the gate. As if it had been dropped by accident. It hadn't been there long or it would have been trodden in or grown over with grass.'

Meg was looking at Art, her head tilted slightly to one side. 'You've got an idea, haven't you?' she said. 'You think you know what happened.'

Art nodded. 'It is just an idea, though.'

'Tell us,' Flinch pleaded.

'I was going to,' Art said, smiling. 'Now, what if this man Quainton did drop the coin that Jennings found? What if he actually had lots of them and just dropped one?'

'Albert Norris said that Jennings heard a sound like coins jangling,' Jonny remembered.

'That's right. So Quainton has these coins from somewhere. He is attacked and knocked down. But when Jennings gets there, the coins have all gone. Except one.'

'Someone stole the coins,' Flinch gasped.

'Someone who wasn't interested in his wallet or snuff box,' Jonny said.

'And then,' Art went on, 'whoever it was must have known where Quainton lived. They know he's out for the count and they ransack the place. Searching for . . .' He stopped, looking round at them, waiting for the answer.

'More of them,' Meg said. 'More Roman coins.'

'Exactly.'

'And they took them,' Flinch realised. 'But they dropped one on the way out of the garden.'

'Which your dad found,' Jonny finished with a grin. 'I think that must be it, Art.'

'There is a treasure,' Flinch said happily. 'We're on a Roman treasure hunt.'

'So what do we do next?' Jonny said. 'There's no point looking at the man's house, and he's dead, poor chap.'

They sat in silence for several moments as they all thought about this. It was Meg who finally spoke.

'When Jennings saw the man,' she said quietly, 'he was frightened and ran off.'

'Doesn't like the police,' Jonny said. 'Lot of people don't.'

'But what if it's more than that? What if he thought he'd been caught?'

'Doing what?' Flinch asked.

'He was caught by someone,' Art pointed out. 'But you're right, Meg. You think he was collecting more of those coins, don't you?'

Meg was nodding. She was smiling too, Flinch saw. 'He's found the treasure,' Meg said. 'But he can't carry it all home in one go, so he leaves it hidden and goes back each night to help himself to another handful of coins.'

'I don't see how that helps,' Jonny said. 'Except that maybe someone else found out about it and killed him to get it for themselves.'

But Art's eyes were shining with excitement. 'Oh, think about it, Jonny! What if he's just come from where the treasure is hidden when he sees a policeman appear out of the fog. That would spook him. He'd run like heck.'

Flinch was beginning to realise what Meg and Art were saying. 'So the treasure's near where the policeman first saw him,' she said.

'Exactly.' Art grinned. 'And we know where that was. By that old graveyard close to the river, down at Northerton, remember?'

'So what now?' Jonny said.

'Well, I quite like Flinch's idea,' Art said.

Flinch frowned. 'What idea?'

Art leaned forward and spoke in a loud, excited whisper: 'Treasure hunt!'

They agreed that they should all be involved in the treasure hunt and that after dark would be the best time. They did not want to attract attention, poking about in a graveyard, so daylight hours were out. But it was not until the weekend that all four of them were free in the evening.

It was easier for Art to get out when his father

was working the night shift. Jonny could slip away fairly easily but had an uncle staying until Friday, so would be missed. Meg was keen that her mother should not be on her own when her father got in from work – or rather, when he got in from the pub, which was where he always went after work. Flinch, of course, could do what she liked, whenever she liked, and got increasingly impatient as the week wore on. Seeing her frustration, Art had to insist Flinch didn't sneak off for a look on her own ahead of their expedition.

'If only it was winter,' Art sympathised on the Friday after school, when they met at the den. 'But it stays light so late in the summer now.'

To Flinch's undisguised disgust, Jonny's uncle had such a pleasant time that he decided to stay another day. So it was Sunday evening before they could all meet at the den after dark and make the short journey to Northerton cemetery. Once again, it was a foggy night. The summer heat seemed to bring the mist off the River Thames like steam. It meant that the night drew in more quickly than usual, but it also made it difficult for Art and the others to find their way. They got lost several times.

Eventually, Art led them to Northerton Avenue, which ran parallel to the river. Halfway along was the cemetery – between the road and the river. They could smell the Thames through the fog, dank and stale.

'Here we are,' Art announced.

He paused by the gate that led through the iron railings and into the graveyard. The nearest tombstones were visible, poking up through the heavy smog that clung to the ground. It was as if they were standing on a sinister cloud.

'Where do we start?' Jonny wondered.

'It's cold,' Flinch complained.

Despite the fact it was the middle of June, the air was damp and clammy, soaking through their clothes.

'He must have come out of this gate,' Meg said. 'I wouldn't want to climb over those railings. They look like spears.'

She was right, Art thought. A row of spears stood on end in the pavement, held together with long metal rods. Nobody in their right mind would try climbing over that, especially when there was a gate.

Art's hand was actually on the gate, ready to

push it open, when they heard it – a scraping, metallic sound from somewhere inside the graveyard. Art froze, looking round at the fog-smudged faces of his friends.

'What was that?' Jonny hissed.

There was more noise now, before anyone could answer. A jangling, like large chains, and the rough, heavy sound of stone rubbing on stone. And somewhere beneath that, voices – low and surreptitious.

'There's someone else here,' Meg said. 'What are they up to?'

'No good,' Flinch said at once. 'It's the middle of the night. Shouldn't be no one here.'

'We are,' Jonny said nervously.

'That's different,' Art whispered back.

'Whoever they are,' Meg said quietly, 'I think they're coming this way.'

She was right. The scraping and jangling had stopped. But the voices were definitely approaching. Art could hear the measured tread of feet crunching on the gravel path that led from the gate.

'Quick!' he hissed. 'Back along the street. Let's see who it is.'

They ran for the nearest hiding place, though it was difficult enough to see through the gathering fog and the darkness. There was a row of houses backing on to the cemetery and they stood in the shadow of the last house. There was a low wall round the tiny front garden. An old bicycle stood leaning against the house and Jonny almost knocked it over as he dived behind the wall – well ahead of his friends.

'Careful of the bike,' he murmured to the others as they joined him.

Together, they peered over and round the wall to see who came out of the graveyard.

It was difficult to make out anything, but dark shapes that could be figures emerged from where Art estimated the gate must be. They were moving slowly and it took him a moment to realise that they were carrying something – barely more than a grey blotch in the fog. There was a heavy metallic sound – jangling, clinking – as they walked. They were talking in low voices, but Art could make out none of the words.

Almost at once, the figures were followed by more, again carrying a long box. Art swallowed as he considered what it might be.

'Grave robbers!' Flinch whispered close to his ear, and he did not hurry to disagree.

'Or maybe they've found the treasure,' Meg said.

'Let's try and get a closer look,' Jonny suggested. He stood up, moving round the wall cautiously.

But not cautiously enough. He caught the bike's pedal with his foot. He scrabbled to catch the bike as it overbalanced, pulling away from the wall of the house, but succeeded only in pulling it down on top of himself. There was a clatter of wheels, the sound of the bike falling and Jonny's surprised cry as he fell. Then the bell rang, loud and clear, as it hit something.

'Well done, Jonny,' Meg said quietly in the sudden silence that followed.

'Help me, then,' he hissed back, struggling to push the bike away without making any more noise.

But the damage had been done. The men emerging from the graveyard were talking more loudly now, calling to others to hurry up.

'Think they'll come looking for us?' Jonny asked nervously as he finally escaped from under the bike.

'No, they're running off,' Flinch said.

'Which proves they're up to no good,' Art pointed out.

'That's something,' Meg admitted, glaring at Jonny. 'I suppose things can't get any worse now.'

At which point the door of the house was flung open by a middle-aged man in striped pyjamas and a threadbare dressing gown. His greying hair was a frizzy mess and he looked far from happy.

'What the bloomin' 'eck's goin' on 'ere?' he yelled. Then he caught sight of Jonny, standing startled in the light from the hallway of the house. 'Kids! I've 'ad enough of kids and noises and people larkin' about in the middle of the bloomin' night, I 'ave.'

He took a step towards Jonny, his arm raised, ready to lash out at him. Flinch had disappeared, and Art and Meg slipped round the wall and out into the street. Jonny hesitated only a moment, then he turned and ran.

'Git off owt of it!' the man shouted. 'I'll 'ave the law on you, so I will.'

He stood framed in the doorway for a moment, his frizzed hair shimmering in the light

41

as he seethed, so that it looked as if his head was on fire. Then he went back inside and slammed the door.

Flinch laughed. 'He was angry,' she said. 'Did you hear him?'

'I should think most of London heard him,' Meg told her.

'And I should think Jonny's halfway back to the den by now,' Art added, amused. But he led them the other way along the street, back towards the gate into the graveyard. 'Jonny and the shouting scared those men off too,' he observed. 'I wonder what they were really doing.'

'Grave-robbing,' Flinch said with conviction.

'Don't be silly,' Meg told her.

Art had spotted a shape on the pavement right by the gate. 'They've dropped something. This wasn't here just now.' He stooped to pick it up.

'Is it treasure?' Flinch asked in a hushed voice.

He straightened up and held it out for them to see. It was pale and brittle and about the length of Art's forearm. 'No, not treasure,' he said. 'Maybe you were right, Flinch. This is a bone.'

*

The room full of people who had assembled that Monday night to hear the Invisible Detective speak were not disappointed. There were intakes of breath as Brandon Lake told them that the man PC Jennings had found was called Derek Quainton and he had died of his injuries. Mutters and murmurings as the detective told them the police were treating the matter as murder. There were outright gasps of astonishment when the Invisible Detective mentioned the legend of the Lost Legion and the fact that the coin Jennings had discovered was from the time of Nero and Boudicca.

On the subject of Jennings's glimpse of a Roman soldier, Brandon Lake announced that there was still much to investigate but that the poor policeman's imagination might be responsible for this singular apparition.

Jonny, Meg and Flinch were, as usual, behind the curtains. Flinch had grown bored of the proceedings and was sitting on the floor, tracing patterns in the dust under the window. Jonny was poised, as ever, with his fishing rod, and Meg listened attentively as Albert Norris said thank you for the detective's work on his behalf.

'My old dad used to talk about the legend of the Lost Legion,' he went on. 'He used to say there was talk of the treasure they was paid. Do you think, sir, that the coin I brought last week might be part of that treasure?'

Meg listened all the more carefully for Art's answer to this.

'It is certainly possible,' Art conceded in his artificially deep voice. 'But on the other hand, the story is merely a legend and a single Roman coin is hardly a treasure save to historians. Having said that,' he went on, 'I do believe that there is at least one other coin of a similar sort that has recently been turned up.'

There was renewed interest at this. 'You reckon there's more of them? A whole pile of coins waiting to be dug up?' someone called out.

'Reckon it'd be near where that bloke Quainton lived, then,' another voice said.

'Use your head, Gerry. It'll be near the graveyard at Northerton where Quainton died, won't it?' chimed in a third voice.

Meg found herself feeling disappointed that they had reached this conclusion so quickly. It made it seem so obvious.

'It ain't there,' a new voice said. It came from close to the curtain.

'How d'you know that, whoever you are?' Albert Norris demanded.

'I know because I knew Derek Quainton. That's how.'

Meg was listening closely. This could be important. She was conscious of Jonny quivering with excitement close to her. Flinch had stood up and joined them.

'Didn't know him well, mind,' the man went on. 'Just to talk to in the street when I saw him about the place. And he showed me that coin he found.'

Through the crack in the curtains, Meg could just make out the form of the man who was speaking. Even in the gloom of the dimly lit room she could see that he was dressed in grubby, ill-fitting clothes and looked as if he had not brushed his hair or shaved for a week or more.

'Perhaps you could tell us what you know,' the Invisible Detective suggested. 'Please also tell us a little about yourself.'

The man sniffed. 'Not a lot to tell. I live locally.'

'On the local streets, more like,' someone said.

There were several stifled laughs at this.

'Nothing wrong with living rough on the streets if you have to,' he snapped back.

Flinch was nodding in agreement as she listened. But Meg was frowning. There was something not quite right here. The man wasn't lying, but there was something that didn't ring true about his story.

'Anyway, I knew Quainton and I knew he had found some old coins. What's more, I know where, and it wasn't buried in any old graveyard.'

As the man stabbed his finger in the air to make his point, Meg could see he was wearing a ring. It was illuminated, just for a second, in the pale glow of the table lamp. A large, dark ring with a silver pattern on it. She could not make out what it was, because his hand moved so fast.

'Where was it, then, clever-clogs?' a voice demanded.

'I'm not telling. It'll be a circus if I say where there might be treasure. You'll all be down there in a shot like kids at the seaside with your buckets and spades.'

There was renewed laughter at this. Art's deepened voice cut across it.

'I think you have a good point, sir,' he said. 'So may I suggest that you disclose this secret location to someone in authority who can then take the appropriate action?'

'Ain't going to the peelers,' the man insisted. 'And anyway,' he confessed in a voice that was little more than a mutter, 'I only knows the general area. The locale. Nothing exact.'

'Even so,' the detective said, 'the right and proper thing to do would be to go to Mr Worthington, who is the curator of the Myton Museum near here, and tell him all about it. Worthington will know whether this locale, as you put it, is likely to be a hiding place for the treasure of the Lost Legion. Though I should warn you all that the treasure, like the single coin, may only be valuable to collectors or to historians like Mr Worthington.'

There was a pause while the man considered this. 'All right,' he decided. 'I'll tell this Worthington fellow. I'll do it right away. Then you can all forget about Northerton cemetery, cos there's no lost treasure there, I can tell you.'

As he turned and strode purposefully from the room, Meg pulled at Jonny's sleeve.

'What?' he whispered. 'You want to tell Art something? Was he lying?'

'I don't know.' Meg could hear the man's feet on the stairs. 'He wasn't really lying. But there's something wrong. I think you should get to the museum and make sure he tells Worthington what he knows.'

Jonny looked at the fishing rod, then back at Meg. On the other side of the curtains, someone was asking about a missing dog. 'If it's open this late. Anyway, why me?'

Meg took hold of the fishing rod. 'Because Worthington knows you best,' she hissed. 'And because you're the only one who can get there before the other man does and be ready when he arrives.'

'Oh,' Jonny said. 'Right.' He let go of the rod and went to the end of the curtain. After a quick check that no one was standing just the other side of it, he slipped out and was gone.

Pretending to be interested in a model showing how roofs are thatched, Jonny listened carefully to the conversation between the man, who had identified himself as Mr Orton, and Worthington. Jonny had arrived, breathless, at the museum just as Worthington was locking the door. He persuaded the curator to open up on the pretext of important homework from school that he had to finish for tomorrow.

Within a couple of minutes, Orton arrived. He looked dishevelled and dirty, his clothes torn and stained, and his face and hands ingrained with dirt. His whole manner and appearance were almost theatrical, Jonny thought – like someone playing a tramp in a film. Except for the ring.

Perhaps that was left from a previous life. The finger had swelled round it as the man put on weight, and Jonny doubted he could take it off to sell or pawn. It was black, with a design in silver showing two snakes intertwined, their heads poised ready to bite at each other. Jonny couldn't recall having seen another ring like it. It was obviously well crafted, but there was something unsettling and a little grotesque about it too.

The ring was soon forgotten as Jonny listened and watched. He was amused by how animated and enthusiastic Worthington became as a result of Orton's story. He was almost bouncing on his feet, reminding Jonny a little of Flinch when she was excited.

'And where was it?' Worthington asked at last. 'Where did Quainton say he found this coin? The Northerton area would certainly fit with what we know about Roman barracks and troop placements at the time.'

'Weren't anywhere near Northerton,' Orton said, shaking his head emphatically. 'Miles away.'

'Then where?'

Jonny had given up all pretence now and was standing watching and listening quite openly.

'Stepney,' Orton said.

Worthington's mouth dropped open. 'Stepney?'

'Near Stepney Green. Hawthorne Crescent Gardens,' he said.

'Stepney?' Worthington said again. 'But that wouldn't fit with what Tacitus tells us at all. It's a good couple of miles from where he suggests the legion was last seen.'

Orton shrugged. 'Well, I said I'd tell you and now I've told you. So the Invisible Detective should be well chuffed.'

Worthington did not seem to hear. 'Stepney?' he said again, his voice quiet and incredulous as Orton stomped off out of the museum.

Jonny lingered only a moment. 'Disappointed?' he asked.

'Well . . .' Worthington sighed. 'It can't be the Lost Legion's treasure. But then again, I suppose I never really believed in it anyway. Shame, though.' He sighed again. 'Yes, great shame.'

'Maybe he's wrong, or misheard.'

Worthington nodded absently. 'Probably lying drunk in a gutter when this chap told him. Can't really rely on his memory.'

'No,' Jonny agreed.

Somehow he felt Meg had a point – there was something not quite right about Mr Orton. He was trying to work out what it could be as he let himself out of the museum.

As he closed the door behind him, Jonny could hear Worthington's voice, quiet and almost lost in the large room. Just one word: 'Stepney?'

The sun was dipping behind the buildings opposite, making their shadows long enough to shade the whole street. Jonny stepped out into the last of the sunlight, dazzled for a moment. But after two steps he was in shadow, and he could see Orton further down the road.

A car had stopped beside Orton and the scruffy man was talking to the driver through the window. It was a cab. Jonny could tell from the slightly higher roof and the missing front passenger seat – to give more space for luggage. Jonny watched, surprised. It was unusual for a cab driver to have to stop and ask directions; most of them knew the streets of London like the back of their hand.

Jonny stepped into the doorway of the museum. The sun had slipped that bit further and he was no longer dazzled by it. Orton was fumbling in his pocket for something. He had raised his voice angrily, though Jonny couldn't catch what he said. He showed something to the cab driver, who shook his head. But it seemed to be in surprise rather than disagreement now. And, to Jonny's astonishment, he reached behind and pushed open the back door of the vehicle to allow Orton to climb in.

A scruffy vagrant – a tramp – getting into a taxi? No wonder the driver had wanted to see some cash before letting him in. It was a surprise he had stopped at all. Jonny watched the cab pull away from the kerb, turn in the street and head off. Meg had been right – there was something strange about Mr Orton, and Jonny was determined to find out what it was.

A cab was actually easier to follow than a car. The driver might know more of the short cuts and back alleys, but with a fare they tended to keep to the main streets. More importantly, they travelled more slowly as a rule. The standard licensed cab actually had inferior brakes – deliberately so. The reasoning was that a cab driver who knew his brakes weren't as good as they could be would be inclined to drive more slowly and carefully. And Jonny knew that more often than not this was indeed what happened.

He was in a part of the city he knew well and that helped too. He could anticipate where the cab would go and take short cuts. He knew the little paths and alleys between the blocks of houses, the ways out of dead ends, the ways through small parks . . . He followed the cab for perhaps two miles, glimpsing it at street corners and hoping Orton did not spot him.

Eventually, just as Jonny was beginning to think his lungs would burst if he didn't stop for breath, the cab drew up outside a house. Hands on his knees and panting hard, Jonny watched from the other side of the road. They were in a crescent of large Regency town houses – tall and imposing. Not the sort of area where one would expect to see a man like Orton. So Jonny watched with interest as the dishevelled man paid off the cab and started up the steps to one of the houses.

The cab blocked Jonny's view for a moment as it pulled away. Then he could see Orton standing in the doorway. The door had been opened by a tall man in a suit – the butler. Jonny waited for the butler's face to betray his surprise and distaste, waited for the door to be slammed shut, leaving Orton standing on the steps outside.

But instead the butler nodded deferentially and stepped back to allow the scruffy, grubby man into the house. The door closed behind him, leaving Jonny watching open-mouthed in surprise.

They had been talking about it all day at school. Some of the girls were talking about nothing else, or so it seemed to Arthur. But he hadn't expected Sarah to be so interested.

They often walked part of the way home together, even though she was in the year above him. She had long black hair and a pretty, oval face with a nose that turned up just slightly at the end.

It wasn't because she looked good that Arthur liked to be with her, though. Well, not just that. Sarah Bustle was the only other person who knew about the Invisible Detective. Her father had told her stories about Brandon Lake, though neither Arthur nor Sarah was sure quite how he came to know them.

Arthur was keen to talk about the casebook, to tell Sarah how sad it was that the adventures seemed to be ending. OK, it was just a book, but he always hated finishing a good book, even though he was desperate to know what would happen.

But Sarah, like the others, was caught up in the hype and the media coverage. Why couldn't she see what was so obvious to Arthur?

'He's a complete loony,' Arthur told her.

'Oh, he's not. It's a brave thing to do. No one

else has ever done anything like it. That's what they were saying on the news last night.'

Arthur kicked a stone off the pavement into the road. It skittered under a parked car. 'No one's done it before because it's daft. He'll starve or drown or both.'

'You're being daft now. They've got cameras down there.'

'Yeah. And paying a fortune for the TV rights. Anyway, who's going to want to switch on to see a man in a glass box. What's he going to do for a week down there? Apart from eat and sleep and . . .' He shook his head and sighed at the thought. 'And they won't show *that*, thank goodness. Well, maybe on the webcam . . .'

'It's an endurance test,' Sarah told him. She was sounding miffed.

'It's not an intelligence test, that's for sure. Which is probably good, because, I'm telling you, Martin Michael would fail.'

'You're just jealous because he's such a hunk.'

Arthur hadn't expected her to say that. 'I'm a celebrity stuntman-magician, get me in a glass box under the Thames,' he grumbled. 'He's not doing it because it's big or clever. He's doing it because he's got a new DVD or TV series coming out or something.'

They walked on in silence for a minute. Then Arthur said, 'Anyway, I'd rather have two brain cells to rub together than be a hunk.'

Sarah nodded, but she didn't look at him. 'Only two?'

Arthur thought she was trying not to smile.

CHAPTER THREE

The others were waiting back at the den for Jonny.

'Where's the treasure? Did he say?' Flinch demanded as soon as Jonny arrived.

'Let him catch his breath,' Meg told her.

'You were a long time,' Art said. 'Longer than just getting to the museum and back.'

'That's right,' Jonny said. And he told them his story.

'I said there was something odd about that man,' Meg announced when Jonny had finished.

'A tramp who keeps company with the rich and famous,' Art said. 'Well, rich, anyway. We don't know who lives there.'

'Perhaps we should find out,' Jonny suggested.

Art nodded. 'There are a few things we need to find out. That is certainly one of them.'

'What are the others?' Flinch wanted to know. She sounded ready to go and get the answers right away.

'I'd like to know who welcomes scruff-bags Orton into their posh home,' Art said. 'If he really is a "scruff-bags", that is. And whether any more counterfeit money has turned up.'

'Or any more Roman coins,' Meg put in.

'And what those men were up to last night,' Jonny said. 'Where's that old bone, by the way?'

'Is it from a body?' Flinch asked, excited.

'It's down here,' Art said, producing the bone from beside the roll of carpet he was sitting on. 'And yes, it's from a body. But whether it's a human body or some animal I don't know. We'd have to ask an expert. Like a doctor or someone.'

'Or Charlie,' Flinch suggested.

Charlie – or Lord Fotherington, to give him his proper title – was a friend of theirs, and treated them to tea and cake at the café at the railway station every Tuesday afternoon.

'We'll see him for tea tomorrow, won't we?' she went on.

'I don't know,' Art told her. 'He was away last week, remember? I'm not sure if he'll be back yet.'

'Oh.' Flinch looked disappointed.

'But when he is we shall have lots of clues to share with him, I'm sure,' Art said.

Flinch brightened at this. 'Maybe we'll find the treasure, now we know where it is.'

'Stepney, or so Orton claims,' Jonny said.

'But Mr Worthington didn't seem to think that was likely.'

'So where do we start?' Meg asked. 'I'll need to get home soon.'

'How soon?' Art asked her. 'What I mean is, do you and Flinch have time to make a quick call on Mr Orton's posh friends tonight?'

Flinch jumped to her feet, ready to go at once. 'I bet I could get into that house,' she said. 'Through a window or something. It don't have to be open much. Then I could let Meg in and we could look for clues. Maybe they're keeping him prisoner there.'

Art and Jonny laughed. Even Meg smiled.

'What?' said Flinch.

'He went there of his own accord,' Jonny said. 'He's not going to be a prisoner.'

'Oh.' Flinch sat down again.

'And there may not be any clues. They've done nothing wrong,' Art said. 'Except let a tramp into their house. Maybe he's a distant and disreputable relative or something.'

'Oh.'

'It would be useful to know who lives there, that's all,' Meg said.

'Oh. How do we find that out?'

'It's not far,' Meg decided. 'I've got time if we go now. We'll say we're doing a survey for school, or collecting for a charity, or looking for Mr Smith or something.'

'Obtaining information,' Art said to Flinch. 'That's proper detective work.' Flinch beamed, and Art smiled back. 'And Jonny and I will be doing some minor detective work of our own.'

'Will we?' Jonny said. 'What?'

'I thought we'd pay a quick visit to the Dog and Goose. Get the local gossip.'

'Pubs,' Meg muttered, disapproving.

'Traditionally, they're a good place to listen out for the latest information about fake money and Roman treasure,' Art told her.

The evening was drawing in as Meg and Flinch arrived at the street Jonny had described. The houses were painted white, but they looked almost pink in the last of the sun. The lamps were not yet lit, so the street was a twilight of shadows.

'Now, you let me do the talking,' Meg said to Flinch for the third time. She doubted it would make any difference, though. If Flinch wanted to say anything, she would go ahead and say it regardless.

But Flinch nodded, biting her bottom lip slightly nervously as they approached the house. 'What are you going to say?'

Meg wasn't actually sure. 'We'll see. Depends who comes to the door.'

It was the butler Jonny had described. He looked down his nose at the girls and sniffed. 'Are you lost?' he asked after several moments.

'Course not,' Flinch told him, and Meg nudged her with her elbow.

'We're looking for Mr Toplodies,' she said.

'I thought it was Smith,' Flinch hissed.

Meg ignored her. She had been going to ask for Mr Smith, but then it occurred to her that the owner of the house, or even one of the servants, might actually be called Smith and that could be embarrassing.

'I beg your pardon,' the butler said. 'Miss,' he added as an afterthought.

'Mr Toplodies,' Meg repeated, hoping she would remember the absurd name she had thought of. 'Isn't this his house? I know he lives along here somewhere.'

The butler was shaking his head. He pushed the door closed. 'No one here of that name,' he said.

'What name, then?' Meg said desperately as the door continued to close. 'Who does live here?'

'Not Mr Toply-whatzit, that's who.'

The door was almost shut. Meg gave Flinch a despairing look. Flinch also looked disappointed. They had failed.

'Sorry,' Meg mouthed. She knew Art would tell them it didn't matter, but knowing that just made it worse somehow.

The door started to open again. There was someone else standing with the butler now. A tall, thin man in a brown suit. He had the thumb of one hand hooked into his waistcoat pocket. His other hand was pushed into his trouser pocket, so that he looked confident and relaxed. His face was round and slightly pudgy.

'I'm sorry about Carstairs,' he said, his voice rich and deep. 'I gather you are looking for someone?'

'Mr Toplodies,' Meg said quickly. 'Is he here?' she added hopefully.

'I'm afraid not. In fact I know no one of that

name. But perhaps if you could describe him I might be able to help. I might have seen him about and not known who he is.'

'He's quite short,' Flinch said.

At the same moment Meg said, 'He's a tall man.'

They both stopped and looked at each other. The man in the doorway regarded them with amusement.

'Actually,' Meg said, nudging Flinch again to be quiet, 'we haven't met him before. We don't know what he looks like.'

'He's a chimney sweep,' Flinch said, which surprised Meg almost as much as it surprised the man. 'We thought you might be him.'

'Me? Oh, no no no.' The man smiled. He pulled his hand out of his pocket and waved it dismissively in the air. 'I have a rather more ordinary name. And occupation. Though I shouldn't be surprised if we don't need the chimneys swept.' He turned to the butler, who was standing behind him in the hallway. 'Carstairs?'

'Indeed, sir. I shall make arrangements. The usual man is called Johnson, but I gather he's recently retired.'

'Well,' the man said to Meg and Flinch, 'if you find your Mr . . . your man, then send him along here. We may have some work for him.'

Meg nodded. She didn't know what to say to that. They still didn't know the name of the man and she could hardly ask him outright. But they did know something. She was staring at the man's hand. One part of the mystery at least was solved.

'You sure you're not him?' Flinch said. 'You look like a sweep to me. Can I touch you for luck?'

The man laughed. He held out his hand. 'If you like. But I assure you I have never swept a chimney in my life. My name is Augustus Bablock and I run a printing works, if you must know. I'm not sure it's lucky to touch a printer, though I dare say both printers and sweeps will leave your hands black if you're not careful.'

'Thank you,' Meg said. Suddenly she didn't want to stay here any longer than she had to. 'We must have got the wrong address. I'm sorry.'

She led Flinch down the steps and along the street.

'He was nice,' Flinch said.

'Yes,' Meg said, but she didn't sound convinced.

'You didn't think so?' Flinch stared at Meg. 'Was he lying?'

'No, he wasn't lying. But now we know who he is, and we know why Orton was let into the house.'

'We do?'

'You saw his hand,' Meg said. 'His ring.'

'With the snakes?'

They had both seen it clearly – a large dark ring, with an emblem engraved on it in silver. Two snakes, intertwined, each about to bite at the other.

'It's the same ring as that tramp Orton was wearing.'

Flinch gasped. 'They stole his ring? They've murdered him and taken his things!'

Meg tried not to laugh. 'No, Flinch,' she said gently. 'Tramps don't have "things". But people who live in houses like that do. It's Bablock's ring. I didn't realise till I saw the ring, but then I could tell. There's no such person as Orton. It was Bablock dressed up.'

'But why?'

'I don't know,' Meg admitted. 'Another mystery.'

The Dog and Goose on a Monday night was not terribly busy. Neither Art nor Jonny was inclined to linger. They were in disguise, true, but all that really meant was that they had the collars of their coats turned up and their caps pulled down low over their eyes. They knew from past experience that this was going to attract attention if they stayed too long – especially in the middle of summer, though the cold turn the weather had recently taken would help. It was becoming easier to spend time in the pub as they got older and taller, but they still needed to take care not to be spotted.

The conversation at the bar was hardly inspiring. Art and Jonny each had a half of bitter, which neither of them drank. It seemed a waste of the pennies that the Invisible Detective collected to help Flinch, but it was all in a good cause, Art reminded himself. They raised the glasses to their lips, and tried to tip some beer away – letting it dribble and splash to the floor or the top of the bar when no one was looking.

Art had hoped that if they hung around, sooner or later someone would ask Albert Norris if he'd been passed any more dud money. Or any Roman coins. But tonight no one seemed much interested in anything apart from dog racing.

'This isn't helping,' Jonny said quietly.

'I know,' Art replied.

'Maybe we should ask Albert ourselves,' Jonny suggested.

'Don't want to attract attention,' Art told him.

Jonny grinned at that. 'He might call your dad to arrest us.'

Art didn't find that so funny. It was horribly possible. Perhaps they should just give up and admit that they were not going to find anything out.

'I suppose,' Art said, trying to justify this, 'that if no one's mentioned it, then nothing's happened. No more counterfeit money and no more Roman treasure.'

He was facing Jonny, turned away from the bar, so he did not see that Albert Norris was reaching for a glass right next to Art as he spoke.

'Roman treasure you're after, is it?' he said loudly, close to Art's ear. Art jumped, and Norris laughed. 'Yeah, well, we sell Roman treasure by the pint here, you know.'

'Like prawns,' someone further along the bar shouted out. 'And speaking of prawns, I reckon we've a quart of them in here tonight and all.' He let out a massive guffaw.

'What d'you want to know about Roman treasure, then?' Norris demanded as he pulled a pint.

Art shrugged. 'We just heard how you'd found a Roman coin or something,' he said, trying to make his voice sound gruff and older.

Norris nodded, apparently satisfied with this. 'S'right. Wasn't found in here, though. No, they reckon there might be some treasure somewhere. Northerton, wasn't it?' he asked the man who had joked about prawns.

'No,' the man said. 'Northerton's old news. Henry Beatty reckons it's over in Stepney now. He was talking to that vagrant before the detective's session tonight and got the low-down.' He bellowed with laughter again. 'Mike Hodges and Archie Finnegan were going over there tonight with shovels till Maddie put the spooks into them.'

'So Orton's told everyone anyway,' Jonny muttered to Art.

'Seems so,' Art murmured back, still listening.

'What's Maddie been telling them?' Norris wanted to know.

'She says the last couple of nights there's been talk of ghosts round Stepney Green, right where that fellow said the coins were found.'

'Ghosts?' Art said out loud.

'Yeah. Spooks. Spirits. Apparitions.' He gave a ghostly laugh and waved his hands in the air to demonstrate.

'Clanking chains and all, is it?' someone suggested.

'Nah,' the man said, looking down into the remains of his pint. 'Roman soldier, Maddie says. Marching up and down, glowing like something out of hell's pit. Guarding the treasure that probably ain't there anyway.' He drained his glass and slammed it back down on the bar. 'You know what Maddie's like.'

Art nudged Jonny. They had discovered all they were likely to, and it seemed the evening had not been wasted after all. Together they shuffled slowly towards the door, heads down, hoping not to be noticed.

'Don't you want to drink up?' Norris called after them. He was frowning as Art glanced back. 'How old are you two anyway?'

Jonny kept asking the time, but Art knew he was more nervous about seeing a ghost than about getting home. It was late, but he had been out later – much later – before now. Art's father was still working the night shift at Scotland Yard, so Art was in no hurry either.

'I mean, it's just a story, isn't it?' Jonny said.

'Oh, no,' Art said. 'There have been reported sightings of the ghostly Roman soldier of Stepney since the Middle Ages.'

'Really?' Jonny's mouth was hanging open.

'It's said to stalk its victims through Stepney Green, sword raised ready to strike. Either they die of shock or . . .' He was keeping his face turned away so that Jonny could not see his expression.

'Or?' Jonny's voice was a hoarse whisper.

'Or they die laughing,' Art said. Unable to

control himself any longer, he almost collapsed with hysterics.

Jonny just looked at him. 'Oh, very funny. That makes me feel much better.' But then he too started to laugh, and before long they were both staggering along the street, bent almost double.

It was a good twenty-minute walk to Stepney. Jonny had a rough idea where Hawthorne Crescent Gardens was – he had cut through there once running from . . . He was vague about what he had been running from. 'Just running,' he said when Art asked him.

Hawthorne Crescent was a curved street of town houses that formed almost a semicircle. There was only one side to the street and opposite was a small area of parkland, complete with a little wood at the top of a shallow rise. It had been rather neglected recently – the grass was up to the boys' knees, the paths, such as they were, overgrown. The undergrowth beneath the trees made it almost impossible to get in among them.

'I dunno why they call it gardens,' Jonny said, looking round.

The whole area was fenced off, but they had

found a gate. It opened soundlessly under Art's hand.

'Well, someone bothers to oil the gate, even if they don't cut the grass or do the weeding,' he commented. 'Be a good place to hunt for treasure,' he went on, looking round. 'Flinch would love it.'

'Where do we start?' Jonny wondered.

'Just look out for the ghostly Roman soldier and see where he's standing,' Art told him.

'Yeah, right. You think he's guarding the treasure.'

'Could be,' Art said. He followed it with a ghostly laugh – a good imitation of the man in the pub.

'Let's try towards the wood,' Jonny said. 'If there was treasure just lying about in the grass, someone would have found it by now, ghost or no ghost.'

'Perhaps we should split up to search,' Art said, half seriously. But Jonny's pained expression made him laugh again and they headed up a slight incline towards the trees together, sticking to what might once have been a path where the grass seemed a little thinner.

'We'll just have a quick look round,' Art said, 'then get off home. All right?'

Jonny nodded. The further they went from the road, the less light there was. Art had not realised quite how dark it had become. There was no moon and the clouds were lying thick across the sky in grey-black patterns. He had thought to bring a torch, but its pale beam only illuminated a few feet ahead of them before it was lost in shadows.

'What are we looking for?' Jonny asked.

'Any sign of where that Quainton fellow might have found his coins. I think you're right, they're not likely to be lying around in the grass, so it must be in the wood or beyond it. Look for anywhere that someone might have been recently.'

Jonny stopped abruptly, about ten yards from the nearest tree.

'Yes,' Art said, seeing where the grass had been flattened and the undergrowth pushed aside. 'You're right. It looks as if someone's forced their way through there. Possibly several people.'

But Jonny was shaking his head. 'Not that,' he said. His voice was a jangle of nerves. He raised his hand and pointed to the darkest shadows beneath the trees, off to their right. 'There, look. Something moved. I think there's someone there.'

Art peered into the darkness of the wood. He could see nothing. He switched off the torch and pushed it back into his coat pocket. Probably just Jonny's nerves getting the better of him. 'I can't see anything,' he said. 'Maybe a trick of the light.'

'What light?' Jonny retorted.

'A reflection of my torch, perhaps.'

But even as Art spoke, they both saw the gleam of something moving among the trees. Art thought at first it was another torch. But it was not throwing out a beam – it was simply a glow. Moving. Coming through the trees towards them.

'I don't like this,' Jonny said, clutching at Art's arm.

'Nor me,' he agreed, and his own voice was trembling now.

The Roman soldier burst out from the trees. He stood staring at Art and Jonny, his face gleaming unnaturally in the darkness. Light seemed to emanate from the strips of metal armour over his shoulders, from his breastplate, from his helmet. And from the sword he held stiffly in his right hand. With an ear-splitting cry of belligerence, the soldier raised the sword high in the air, angling it so that it pointed directly at Art and Jonny.

And charged.

There was nothing on the telly. Well, nothing apart from the endless coverage of Martin Michael spouting nonsense about human endurance and stamina and the mysteries of the human mind and body before being sealed inside a glass tank and dropped in the river.

Arthur watched it through on the evening news. Dad was working – the night shift at Scotland Yard – so Arthur was on his own. He picked without much interest at a supermarket pizza that was going cold. He'd overcooked it and the base crunched noisily as he ate. The cheese had gone almost black and it was no longer possible to tell what had been embedded in it. Maybe it was ham.

There was a large crane set up on the Embankment. Its arm dangled a chain that was attached to a hook in the top of the box Martin Michael had climbed inside. The door in the front of the glass tank was sealed shut and the commentator made the rather obvious point that, just as when he had been dumped on top of Mount Everest the previous summer, Martin Michael was on his own now. They tested the tank was air- and watertight by measuring the pressure inside when they attached the air hose.

As the tank was lifted, Arthur could see the little cameras mounted at each corner, staring in and relaying images by wires that ran into the central umbilical. This was a thick tangle of cables threaded through the chain holding the box. The crane would stay attached, constantly manned, the TV man said. So that Michael could be raised out of the Thames at a second's notice if anything went wrong. He made it sound very dramatic and dangerous. Arthur yawned.

He had definitely had enough, he decided. And not just of the pizza. He tipped the remains into the kitchen bin. It was a warm evening, so maybe he'd go for a walk before it got too late, before the light faded.

Arthur's first idea was to call on Sarah. But she

would be glued to the TV, or maybe Michael's glass tank website. He didn't fancy sitting there while she ogled the screen. 'The man isn't even a real magician,' he said out loud. 'It's all stunts and camera tricks.'

As the evening cooled, so a mist developed. Not thick, but enough to smudge the view. It had not been difficult to decide where to go. Having read some more of the casebook, Arthur had decided to go and see if the graveyard at Northerton was still there. It was odd seeing how things had changed since Grandad wrote his notes. The Myton Museum was another place Arthur could check up on. Probably a block of offices or a mobile phone shop by now . . .

It was a pleasant walk. The city seemed quiet for a change. Maybe Martin Michael really was that popular and everyone was at home watching. At least he had escaped from that.

Except, he realised, he had not. The light was beginning to fade as he found himself at the cemetery. It looked almost exactly as he had imagined from Art's descriptions and the rough pencil sketch in the casebook. But what he had not expected was that, as he entered the small graveyard, he had a good view up the Thames. Even in the fading light and gathering mist, Arthur could see the huge crane standing further down the river. The chain and cables from its arm dangled in, as if it was some huge industrial bird sucking up water.

Following the narrow, overgrown path, Arthur soon reached a little mausoleum. The gates were rusted and one had slipped off its hinge. They were chained and padlocked together, just as they had been seventy years before. Beyond that he could see the distant, vague shape of what might be the tomb that the casebook described. The mist hugged the ground, so that the gravestones seemed to be standing in smoke.

And, out of the smoke, a man appeared. He must have walked round from behind the mausoleum while Arthur was staring into the distance, trying to make out the tomb.

'Hello,' Arthur said, hoping to mask the fact that he was startled.

The man nodded. Although he was standing quite close, it was difficult to make out his features. The mist seemed to shroud him so that he became indistinct.

'Hello,' he replied. His voice was deep and

sonorous, and even in that one word Arthur could hear a pronounced accent, though he couldn't immediately place it.

'I was just . . . looking,' Arthur explained.

'You know someone buried here?'

'No. Well, not really. Just out for a walk. What about you?'

'I live here,' the man replied. 'I hope you find what you are looking for.' He turned and walked into the mist.

'I'm not looking for anything,' Arthur said into the gloom.

There was the sound of a laugh from the other side of the little building. 'We are all looking for something,' the man's voice drifted back. 'Don't you think so, Arthur Drake?'

And, from behind him, a hand closed on Arthur's shoulder.

CHAPTER FOUR

Art and Jonny's cries mingled with the shouts of the soldier who was charging towards them. They turned and ran back down through the parkland towards the gate. The long grass whipped at Art's legs and his speed was hampered by the long coat he was wearing from his disguise. Suddenly he felt his ankle turn as it caught. He hoped he wouldn't fall, hoped he wouldn't twist or sprain it. Hoped the soldier wouldn't reach him.

Jonny, of course, was well ahead, but he seemed to realise that his friend was lagging behind. He slowed, waiting for Art, then grabbed his hand and dragged him onwards.

'Thanks!' Art managed to gasp, before risking a look over his shoulder.

The soldier was still chasing after them, whirling the short sword above his head. He might be an apparition, but his sword looked solid enough to Art.

By the time they reached the gate, the boys had managed to gain some ground. The soldier was still charging down the hill after them, but he was slowing now and his battle cry had subsided into a series of grunts.

'We disturbed his resting place,' Jonny said between deep breaths. 'Now he wants revenge. You think he's guarding the treasure?'

'I don't know,' Art admitted. 'But I'm not waiting to find out.'

'He'll pursue us to the ends of the earth,' Jonny said. He shook his head. 'It's hopeless.'

The soldier was almost on them now. Art could see the man's bare knees beneath his long tunic, the laces holding his armour in place, the helmet straps that linked under his chin. The nose was twisted and broken out of shape – smudged across the soldier's face, like an unlucky boxer's.

'Come on,' Art said.

'There's no escape,' Jonny protested. 'He'll never give up, never tire.'

'Then we need somewhere to hide.'

Art was already looking round. They could try knocking on people's doors. But asking a complete stranger to save them from the ghost of a dead Roman soldier might take some explaining and they didn't have the time. He grabbed Jonny by the shoulder and together they ran along the pavement, doubling back past the gardens.

The soldier saw them and waved his sword angrily. He quickened his pace, heading for the gate.

'You see? He's still after us.'

'Not far now,' Art said.

He'd had an idea. As the soldier reached the gate, they would be hidden from him by the bushes close to the fence. Just for a few moments, until he was through the gate, Art and Jonny had time to hide.

There was a dark shape ahead of them, jutting out into the pavement – a tall square of blackness. Art remembered seeing it as they arrived, though he had thought nothing of it then. He bundled Jonny towards the large box-like structure.

'A police box?' Jonny said in surprise.

'Let's get inside.'

'It'll be locked.'

'Then we'll hide behind it.'

Art could see the familiar dark blue shape of the police box – the stacked roof with its light on top that flashed if there was a message for the policeman on the beat. There was a panel on the door that opened. Behind it was a telephone that would connect them directly to the local police station. The policeman could get into the box itself, to take shelter or call in to the station. Art was hoping the door wasn't locked.

But of course it was. In frustration, he pulled at it with all his might and, to his surprise, the door clicked open. It hadn't been properly latched shut. They tumbled inside gratefully and closed the door.

It was dark and cramped – surprisingly small from the size of the box itself. There was a little desk and a chair pushed under it – Art couldn't see them, but he collided with them. He heard the chair scrape on the floor and felt the edge of the desk dig into his side.

'It's no good,' Jonny whispered. 'Ghosts can walk through walls and doors and stuff.'

'Can they?'

Art felt for the chair and managed to pull it towards the door. There were windows close to the top of the box. The lower panels were frosted glass that you couldn't see out of, but the higher panes were clear. He climbed up on to the chair, feeling it wobble and struggling to keep his balance. On tiptoes, chair rocking beneath him, he could just see out. Could just see the ghostly figure marching purposefully along the pavement towards the police box.

'There he is,' Jonny said close to Art's ear.

The surprise made Art wobble more, and he almost fell. Then he realised that Jonny was standing on the small desk.

'See how he glows,' Jonny whispered in awe.

'If he can walk through walls,' Art whispered back, 'how come he had to use the gate?'

'What?'

'He could have cut us off just by coming through the fence. Child's play to a ghost who can walk through walls. But he came the long way. Why?'

'Habit? Or maybe he doesn't know he can do it.' Jonny's voice was a mixture of anxiety and interest now. 'Maybe he doesn't even know he's dead.'

'Maybe,' Art said.

Outside, the soldier had stopped by the police box. He reached out and rattled the door, but Art had made sure it was properly closed and locked this time. When it didn't open, the soldier walked slowly all round. Art and Jonny twisted and craned to keep him in sight through the windows on the other sides of the police box.

'Or maybe,' Art breathed, 'he isn't a ghost at all.'

'What?'

The soldier pushed his sword into his belt, then reached up and took off his helmet. Underneath, his hair was a tangled, sweaty mess, and the man ran his hand through it. His face was still glowing, but the glow did not extend to his forehead, where it had been covered by the helmet. He gave a sigh and reached into a pouch at his belt with his free hand. Art leaned as far as he dared to see what the soldier was doing.

Bizarrely, he was pulling out a cigarette and a box of matches. Art and Jonny watched in amazement as the soldier pushed the cigarette into his mouth. He struck the match on the side of the police box, let it flare, then lit his cigarette.

'Blooming kids,' he muttered after several drags. Then he shook his head and stamped off into the darkness, swinging his helmet by the chin strap.

'The Romans didn't speak English, did they?' Jonny said quietly.

Art's eyes had adjusted to the gloom enough for him to make out the shape of Jonny clambering down from the desk.

'No, they didn't.' Art too climbed down and fumbled for the lock on the door. 'And I don't think they daubed themselves with luminous paint and smoked cigarettes either.'

'He was pretty convincing, though, wasn't he?' Jonny asked.

'He scared the life out of me,' Art reassured him. 'And he could have done us some serious harm with that sword, ghost or no ghost.'

'But why do it? Why dress up like that and scare people?'

'To keep them away? I don't know.' Art pulled the door of the police box shut behind them. Somewhere in the distance he could hear a tuneless whistling. 'Come on.'

'Where to?'

'Let's follow and see where he goes.'

Jonny hesitated. But only for a moment, then he grinned. 'Yeah, all right. Let's chase him for a change.'

The soldier had not gone far. He was at the other end of the crescent, retrieving a battered holdall from behind a low wall. From inside he pulled a long raincoat, which he put on. He wiped his face on a hanky, still whistling all the time. The glow faded as he rubbed, though there was still a slight aura remaining when he had finished.

Standing in the shadows further along the street, Art and Jonny watched as the man bundled his sword and belt into the holdall and zipped it shut. There was a narrow alleyway down the side of the last of the houses in the crescent. The man disappeared into it. Jonny was about to follow, but Art held him back.

A moment later, the man re-emerged, pushing a bicycle.

'We shan't be able to keep up with that,' Art said.

'You mean you won't,' Jonny told him.

But the man was having trouble. He didn't seem able to organise the holdall so that he could also get on the bicycle. Cursing with frustration, he settled instead for wheeling the bike along, still whistling furiously.

They walked for what seemed like ages, keeping well back and to the darkest part of the streets. The man was in no hurry, it seemed, whistling tunelessly all the while.

'He could have cut through Fosse Lane and been here ten minutes ago,' Jonny grumbled to Art.

'I don't think he knows the area that well,' Art said.

The man seemed to have got lost a couple of times and had had to retrace his steps. Now he was hesitating at a junction ahead of them, deciding which way to go.

'You realise where we are, don't you?' Jonny said after another quarter of an hour.

The night was fairly warm, but a light drizzle was starting to fall and Art was glad of the large coat and his cap. 'No,' he admitted. It was not an area he knew at all. He recognised nothing.

'Well, if he turns left at the end here,' Jonny said, 'that'll take him into Northerton Avenue.'

The rain was getting a little heavier now.

'Where the cemetery is,' Art realised. 'I doubt if that can be a coincidence.'

Sure enough, the man turned into Northerton

Avenue as Jonny had predicted. Halfway down the road, he paused for a few seconds under a streetlamp to light another cigarette, his bicycle propped against the lamp. A gust of wind blew rain into Art's face and he blinked. When he looked again, the man was gone.

'Perhaps he is a ghost,' Art murmured.

Jonny laughed. 'No. He went into the graveyard.'

Art laughed too. 'Friend of ghosts, then. Let's go and see what he's up to.'

Jonny stopped laughing. 'You think that's safe?'

'If we're careful. He doesn't know we're following him. And even if he sees us, we can make a run for it.' Jonny did not seem convinced, and Art punched him gently on the shoulder. 'He scared us half to death, Jonny. I want to know why, don't you?'

'S'pose so.'

'Come on, then.'

They crept quietly into the graveyard. It was not a very big place, so Art reckoned it would not take them long to spot where the man had gone and what he was doing. A single gravel path ran through the graves, snaking its way down towards the other side of the cemetery, where another fence ran along the bank of the Thames. The rain was easing again and the lights from the street threw the gravestones in long, broken shadows.

Art and Jonny made their way cautiously along the path, each of them looking round anxiously in the hope of catching sight of the man with the bicycle. But he was nowhere to be seen. The graveyard was open ground, broken only by the jutting gravestones and the low, dark shape of a mausoleum. They paused beside the little building, but the heavy iron gates across the crumbling entranceway were locked. Rust came off on Art's hands when he pushed at them.

'He's not in there,' Art decided. 'You sure he came in here?'

Jonny nodded. 'I saw him. He was wheeling his bike along this path.'

The only other possible hiding place was a large altar-like tomb: a huge memorial in the shape of a casket, a great slab of stone across its top. Art walked all round one way, while Jonny went the other. They met behind it without seeing another living soul. Moss and lichen grew up the sides of the memorial and ivy trailed across the top. Like the gravestones, it was damp from the rain, visibly darker where the water collected and ran off.

The path ended in a little loop which circled several graves then joined back to itself. The end of the graveyard sloped gently upwards to the fence. At the furthest point there was a good view out across the river. Art could see the black spiky shapes of the cranes at the docks further down. He could make out the slow-moving silhouettes of boats. But beyond the fence was just a low mudflat which was probably covered at high tide. He wondered if the cemetery ever flooded – it seemed lower than the river. But there was no gate, no path, nowhere for a man with a bicycle to have gone.

'We must have missed him,' Jonny said.

'I don't see how we can have done.'

'Let's go back.'

Art agreed. There was no point hanging around waiting for the rain to get worse. 'We can come again in daylight,' he decided. 'Perhaps then we'll be able to see where he went. There must be another gate out of here.'

Jonny was dubious. 'Don't see where. The only way you get out of this place is downwards.' He pointed at the nearest grave and grinned. 'Never heard of anyone having his bike buried with him, though.'

Art laughed at that. 'It's a long walk to heaven,' he said.

From somewhere ahead of them, back towards the road, came a scraping sound. The same sound, Art realised, they had heard here before. He and Jonny both froze. Art nodded to the nearest large gravestone and they ducked behind it.

'What's happening?' Jonny wanted to know.

'No idea,' Art replied. It was instinct rather than knowledge that had made him want to hide.

And sure enough, there were voices now. Just as before. The low, quiet voices of several men. Art peered over the top of the damp gravestone. There, between himself and the gate, two men were walking along the path. They had not been there just now – he was sure of it.

'Where did they spring from?' Jonny whispered.

Art just shook his head. 'Let's follow them.'

'Must we?'

'At least see which way they go,' Art said.

Jonny gave a grunt of disappointment. 'I should get home.' He gave a short laugh. 'Never thought I'd be dying to get *out* of a graveyard,' he said.

Since the two men were heading in the direction of Jonny's house anyway, he couldn't really object to Art's suggestion that they follow. One of the men was tall and thin, the other short and fat. With their hats and their long coats, they reminded Art of Laurel and Hardy at the pictures. He was sure that neither of them could be the Roman soldier who had chased them.

The men seemed to have no idea they were being followed.

'Maybe they don't care,' Jonny said. 'It's not like they've done anything wrong.'

'We don't know what they've done,' Art said. 'Apart from appear out of thin air in the same place as the man we were following – the man who certainly *was* behaving rather suspiciously – vanished.'

'Probably going home to bed,' Jonny grumbled.

Art almost hoped they were. He was getting cold as the night drew in and the rain was keeping up a steady rhythm. It had seeped through his coat and was getting inside his shoes. In front of them, the two men turned into a side street.

'There's nothing down there,' Jonny said in surprise.

'Must be something.'

'There's a factory, or offices or something,' Jonny conceded. 'But nothing else. You can see the houses back on to this street from both sides.'

Art led the reluctant Jonny down the street, past the backs of the houses. At the end was a pair of large wooden gates. The men opened a smaller door in one of them. One of the men had to stoop to get through, the other had to squeeze himself in sideways.

'Bablock Printing Company,' Art read off the gates. The words were painted in large white letters on the dark wood.

'They're just going to work. If they do newspapers and stuff, they probably have to work through the night.'

Art and Jonny drew back into the shadows of the houses as the small door opened again and another man came out. He stood outside the gates, smoking a cigarette and breathing deeply.

'Getting some air,' Art said. 'Probably very hot in there.'

The man flicked the end of his cigarette away. It glowed on the pavement for a moment before fading. He turned to go back inside.

'Come on. Let's get home,' Jonny pleaded. 'There are no clues or anything here.' He stepped out of the shadows and turned to leave.

Art was about to agree when a bell sounded close by. Jonny leaped back as a bicycle swept past, so close to the kerb that the rider almost collided with Jonny on the pavement.

'Blooming kids. They're everywhere,' a voice cursed as the bicycle screeched to a faltering halt outside the gates. It was a voice that Art and Jonny both recognised.

The first man had waited for the bicycle. He held the gate open so the other man could lift it through ahead of him. Their voices carried back to Art and Jonny on the light breeze.

'You been having fun?' the man at the gate asked.

'My knees are perishing cold, I tell you,' the

man with the bike replied. 'It's no fun at all skulking about in those woods waiting for someone to come looking for treasure.'

'Any takers?'

The door was swinging shut behind them, cutting off their voices. Art strained to hear the words of the bicycle man before they were lost.

'Couple of daft kids,' he was saying. 'The story'll be all over London by tomorrow.'

'That'll please the boss.'

Jonny was looking at Art, his eyes wide as he too heard.

'I gave them the fright of their lives, I can tell you.'

The two men's laughter echoed in the still of the night.

Arthur gave a startled cry and spun round. He thought it must be the man he had been speaking to – somehow he had run round the mausoleum and got behind him. But it was a policeman.

'You all right?' the policeman asked.

'Yeah, fine. You made me jump.'

The policeman nodded, as if pleased with himself. 'Wondered what you were up to, wandering round a graveyard talking to yourself.'

'There was a man,' Arthur explained. 'I was talking to him. He just left.'

'Didn't see him. But then the fog's getting up. Gets very foggy down here by the river. This place especially – I suppose because the ground is so low. It slopes right down from the river bank. I reckon we're below the water level here.'

'Really?' Arthur hadn't thought about that, but he could believe it. He had been looking upwards when he saw the crane on the Embankment.

'And the few streets round about. No one comes in here, though, not these days. Except me, checking.' He made it sound like an accusation.

'And the man I saw,' Arthur told him, sounding more defiant than he had intended.

'Maybe. Never seen anyone here. Apart from you, now. What are you doing?'

'Just looking. There's a good view of the crane up the river. The one holding that glass box with Martin Michael in it.'

But the fog had thickened now and the crane

had been swallowed into the approaching night.

The policeman grunted. 'That idiot. Well, we don't want sightseers and fans getting in the way down here.'

'I'm not a fan.'

'It's getting late and it's getting foggy. So I think you'd best be getting off home, don't you?'

'That man,' Arthur said, 'he told me he lived here.'

The policeman looked round and waved his arm in an arc through the mist. 'No one lives *here*,' he said. 'Go on – be on your way.'

CHAPTER FIVE

The dust hung in the air like a thin mist. It made the story that Art and Jonny were telling all the more spooky.

It was Tuesday afternoon and the four of them were back at the den, telling each other of their adventures and discoveries. Flinch shivered as she listened to Art's description of the ghostly Roman soldier who had chased them. She and Meg had already told of their meeting with Bablock, and Art had nodded and smiled the way he did when things were becoming clear to him.

Flinch gasped and clapped her hands together in delight as Jonny told them how the soldier was not a soldier at all, and how he had muttered and lit up a cigarette. Art took up the story again to describe their return visit to the graveyard and then on to the printer's.

'Bablock,' Flinch said when Jonny told them what was on the sign outside. 'That's the same name as the man we met.'

'And he said he was a printer,' Meg added. 'It has to be the same person, doesn't it?'

'It does indeed,' Art said.

'But why?' Jonny asked. 'What's going on?'

'Do you know, Art?' Meg wondered.

'Course he does,' Flinch said. She could tell by the way he was smiling.

'I can make a guess,' Art confessed. 'I think that Bablock has found the Roman treasure.'

'The treasure of the Lost Legion!' Flinch exclaimed.

'Well, maybe not that actual treasure. Mr Worthington at the museum wasn't even sure if it existed. But Roman treasure of some sort. Coins, at least.'

'And he's guarding it with a fake ghost?' Jonny said.

Meg frowned. 'That's more likely to draw attention to it, I'd have thought.'

'Yes, it is, and that's what he wants.'

'What do you mean?' Flinch asked.

'Well, the ghostly Roman soldier has been seen by a few people. Including,' Art said, looking pointedly at Jonny, 'a couple of daft kids who will tell everyone about it. That will make people think there's something going on at Stepney, in those gardens. In that little wooded area.'

'But Mr Worthington said he didn't think that was likely,' Meg recalled.

'It isn't. There's no treasure there at all,' Art explained. 'But now that people know there are Roman coins doing the rounds, they'll want to know where they came from. And suddenly Stepney looks like the best bet. That's where the soldier has been seen. And that is where our scruffy friend Mr Orton says Quainton originally found the coins.'

Meg was nodding. 'And we know that Orton was really Bablock in disguise. He wants everyone to think the treasure is somewhere else.'

'So that he can get on with digging it up in peace and quiet wherever it really is,' Jonny realised.

Art was nodding. 'Of course, we should have known Orton was not who he seemed.'

'I said he wasn't telling the whole story,' Meg said. 'He was telling the truth about knowing where Quainton got the coins from. Only it wasn't where he was telling people.' She sighed. 'If I'd gone with Jonny and heard him tell Worthington, I'd have known he was lying.'

'Never mind,' Art told her. 'We know now.

Anyway, I should have realised when he said he knew the "locale" where the treasure was. What sort of tramp uses a word like *locale*?'

Flinch had listened to all this with interest. But there was one thing she was still desperate to know. 'So where's the real treasure? Where's he digging it up?'

'Well, we can't know for sure,' Art said. 'But from what we've seen, we can make a pretty good guess. Remember those men with wheelbarrows?'

'It's in the graveyard somewhere,' Jonny said quietly. 'Goodness knows where, though. We didn't see it.'

'If it was obvious,' Meg told him, 'it wouldn't have stayed hidden for nearly two thousand years, would it?'

Jonny stuck his tongue out at her and Meg shrugged, her point made.

Flinch was thinking back to the night by the graveyard. 'But they dropped an old bone, not treasure.'

Jonny grinned. 'You go digging in a graveyard and you'll find old bones as well as old coins. They didn't drop it, they probably chucked it away.'

'Are we going to look for the treasure, then?' Flinch demanded. She was on her feet, ready to go.

Art laughed. 'As Jonny says, it must be well hidden. No, I think we'll get expert help.'

'Mr Worthington,' Jonny suggested.

'That's right. Though we might do better to ask him to check out the Stepney site first, to prove there really isn't any treasure there. Then we can tell him about the graveyard and where the policeman first saw Quainton.'

'The museum closes at five,' Jonny told them. 'So we'll need to hurry.'

'Which museum is that?' a voice asked from behind them.

It was a voice that Flinch recognised at once. She turned in delight. 'Charlie! You're back. We didn't hear you come in.'

'I thought we were going for tea at the station café,' Charlie said. He was a tall, thin, elderly man with a mass of energetic white hair that sprang from his head in an unruly fashion. 'It is Tuesday, isn't it?'

'We weren't sure you were coming,' Art said.

'We're just off to the Myton Museum,' Meg

explained. 'We could go for tea afterwards.'

'If we're not too busy digging up buried treasure,' Jonny added.

Charlie smiled, his pale eyes twinkling with interest and amusement. 'It does sound as if you've been having fun while I've been away suffering the boredom of Jonah Grantman's trade negotiations. I can see we're in a hurry, so why don't you tell me all about it as we go?' He led the way out of the storage area. 'I assume this is something to do with your investigations for the enigmatic Mr Brandon Lake.'

Charlie paused as they approached the museum. He pulled out a large white handkerchief and dabbed at his forehead.

'Do forgive me. I seem to have been walking briskly all afternoon.'

'I'm sorry if Jonny was going a bit fast,' Art said, winking at Flinch.

'That wasn't fast,' Jonny complained.

'Really, it is no worry at all,' Charlie said, pushing his handkerchief back into his pocket and leading them onwards again. 'I was delayed on my walk to you, so had to hurry, that's all. I thought

I'd left plenty of time. But there was some sort of commotion round Stepney.'

'Stepney?' Meg said.

'You know it?'

On the way Art and the others had told Charlie about the Roman coins that had been found. But they had not yet mentioned the Roman soldier. Art wanted to ask Charlie what was going on – perhaps someone had caught the fake ghost. But Mr Worthington had emerged from the museum and was locking the door behind him.

'He's early today,' Jonny said. 'Usually he stays late.'

'He does seem in a bit of a rush,' Meg said.

Worthington looked flustered and excited. He finished locking the museum door and turned round to find Art and the others standing in front of him.

'Oh, my word,' he exclaimed, and gave a little jump of surprise that sent his mop of dark hair into a tangle. 'Oh, it's you, and . . .' He looked at Charlie and blinked.

'This is Charlie,' Flinch said. 'He's our friend. We wanted to show him our coin.'

Worthington frowned. 'Oh, um, well . . .' he spluttered.

'Another time perhaps,' Charlie said quickly. 'When you are in less of a hurry.'

'You're very kind,' Worthington replied. 'I was hoping to escape slightly early today, what with all the excitement.'

'What excitement?' Art asked.

'You've not heard? Of course, you wouldn't have.' Worthington was hurrying along the street and they all hastened to keep up. 'I wonder why you can never find a cab when you need one. No, they telephoned me half an hour ago. The most amazing thing. Most unexpected. Just as the, er, scruffy gentleman said, though I must say I never expected him to be right.' He paused and looked at Jonny. 'You remember, don't you? You were there.'

Jonny gaped. 'I don't know what you're talking about.'

'The treasure!' Worthington cried. 'They've found it.'

'In Northerton cemetery?' Art said.

Worthington was nodding rapidly. 'Coins, artefacts, even bodies. Could be the so-called Lost

Legion after all, you know.' He broke off, his enthusiasm turning into a deep frown that lined his forehead. 'Cemetery?' He shook his head. 'No, no, no. Some woodland apparently. In Stepney.'

Jonny laughed. Meg was smiling. Flinch looked confused. But nothing like as baffled as Art was looking.

'Stepney?' he said quietly. 'Hawthorne Crescent Gardens.'

Worthington nodded, brightening again. 'That's the place.'

Jonny clapped Art on the shoulder. 'Well, Art,' he said, 'it seems that for once you were completely wrong.'

Charlie managed to hail a cab in the next street and, to the driver's evident amazement, all six of them piled in.

Art spent most of the journey in silence, deep in thought. But Charlie soon engaged Worthington in a discussion of how best to excavate ancient remains. He mentioned his association with Sir Henry Crichton, the archaeologist, and Worthington launched into a discussion about Crichton's excellent work in Egypt.

'He's just sulking,' Jonny said to Flinch when she asked if Art was all right. 'He doesn't like to be wrong.'

Art looked up briefly at this. 'I don't mind being wrong,' he said. 'But I'm not sure I am, yet.'

The cab dropped them close to the police box where Art and Jonny had hidden just the previous night. Now a chubby policeman was standing in the open door of the box, drinking tea from a chipped enamel mug. Charlie immediately went up to him.

'I am Lord Fotherington and this is Mr Worthington from the Myton Museum,' he announced. 'Perhaps you could direct us to the recent discoveries.'

The policeman hastily downed his tea and lost the mug somewhere inside the box. He pulled the door shut behind him and led them importantly towards the gate into the gardens.

'It's this way, sir.' He glanced at Art and the others but said nothing.

'They're with us,' Worthington assured him. 'Here to help.'

'Of course, sir. Well, Constable Pinning is keeping an eye on things. Bit of a circus, actually.'

'A circus?' Worthington said excitedly. 'You don't mean an amphitheatre?'

'A what?' The policeman looked puzzled. 'I mean with all the people. Most of the public have got bored and moved on, but there's a couple of chaps from the British Museum and a lad from the council with a grand-sounding title though he looks about fifteen years old at most. And old Donald Parry, of course.'

'Who is Donald Parry?' Charlie asked.

'Oh, sorry, sir. He lives just over there.' The policeman pointed. 'Bit of a local character, if you take my meaning.'

The gardens looked no better cared for in daylight than they had the previous night. Art could see where the grass had now been trampled down by many more sets of feet. He wondered if any of the tracks he could make out were those he and Jonny had left when running from the soldier. But of course it was impossible to tell.

The undergrowth at the edge of the wood had also been pushed and broken away. There was a definite path now leading through the trees. As they reached the woodland, Art could see several people standing round talking. A large man with thinning hair and dressed in a heavy tweed jacket was lying on the ground, poking at it with a walking stick. At once Worthington ran to help, with Charlie following close behind.

Flinch was watching in fascination as the men grouped round and began talking. Meg and Jonny were looking at Art, obviously expecting some comment.

'He moved it here,' Art said.

'The treasure?'

'Yes, I was right,' Art went on. 'He needs to shift people's attention.'

'Oh, come on,' Jonny told him. 'You were just wrong about the treasure. I don't know why there's that guy pretending to be a Roman soldier, but the treasure is here all right.'

Charlie had wandered back to join them.

'Isn't it?' Jonny asked him.

'It would seem so. Your friend Mr Worthington is very excited about it all. Though he does say it's been dug over so much by all and sundry that it looks as if it was put there yesterday rather than in the first century.'

Art nodded at this, trying to convey to the others that this was exactly his point.

'Who's the man with the stick?' Flinch wanted to know.

The man in the tweed jacket was now jabbing violently at the ground with his stick, raking up coins. Art could hear them clinking. Worthington was stooped down beside him, trying to tell the man something, evidently frustrated.

'That's the local character,' Charlie said. 'I'm not convinced that he's helping, actually.'

The chubby policeman was now pulling the tweed man reluctantly to his feet and speaking to him in a low voice. He led the man to one side, leaving Worthington and the others to stare down at the excavation and shake their heads sadly.

'Look,' Charlie said, 'I'm sorry to have to ask this, but would you mind terribly if we gave tea a miss for today. Later in the week perhaps?'

'You want to see what happens here,' Art guessed.

Charlie nodded. 'I do. And I want to find a telephone and give Henry a call. He'll love all this. If he's in this country rather than digging up bits of the Middle East, that is.'

'I'm sure that's fine,' Meg told him.

'Provided we still get cake,' Flinch warned.

'Thank you,' Charlie said.

'There's a phone in the police box,' Jonny said. 'Maybe you can use that.'

'You can stay too, of course,' Charlie said.

'Thank you, but we've got something else we need to do,' Art told him. 'We'll see you later.'

Without further explanation, he led the way back down to the gate.

'Where are we going?' Flinch asked.

'You heard what he said, the treasure's been moved here. That's what the men with the wheelbarrows were doing.'

'Moving old bodies too,' Meg said. 'That's why there was that bone.'

'But why?' Jonny was shaking his head. 'It just doesn't make sense. Unless,' he realised, 'there's a whole lot more treasure they're keeping hidden back at the graveyard.'

'And they don't want people looking for that,' Flinch said. 'Is that right, Art?'

'It's possible,' Art said. They had reached the road and he led them towards the reassuring blue shape of the police box. 'I don't know if it's more treasure, but I think there's something in that graveyard that Bablock wants to keep hidden. And he's willing to give up a hoard of Roman coins and valuable artefacts to make sure it stays hidden.'

'But what is it?' Meg demanded. 'What can be worth that much to him?'

'I don't know,' Art admitted. 'Let's go and find out.'

'What, now?'

'Why not?' Jonny said.

'Yes,' Flinch agreed, 'another treasure hunt!'

But Art could see that Meg was not enthusiastic. 'It is getting a little late,' he said, watching for her reaction. He was right.

'I should get home,' Meg said quietly. 'I promised Mum . . .'

'We needn't be long,' Jonny protested.

'You go,' Meg decided. 'You don't want to have to rush things just because of me.'

Jonny looked away and Flinch was staring down at her feet.

'No, we don't,' Art agreed. 'And we need your help, Meg. So we'll leave it until tomorrow.'

'Tomorrow!' Flinch couldn't hide her disappointment. But then she saw Meg's expression. 'Tomorrow,' she repeated, nodding her agreement.

'Straight from school,' Art promised. 'We'll meet at the den, soon as we can. All right?'

'All right,' Flinch said.

Jonny nodded. And Meg smiled.

They met as agreed and went to Northerton. Although it was still the late afternoon and darkness would not fall yet for several hours, Meg could hardly see more than twenty yards. The mist from the river was hanging low over the graveyard. She found the place creepy enough as it was, but with the gravestones mere patches of grey in the gloom, it was even more mysterious and unsettling. She kept close to the others, holding Flinch's hand and hoping the girl didn't realise that it was she who was the more nervous.

'It's spooky,' Flinch declared happily.

'It is rather,' Art agreed. 'I'm afraid we probably won't see much in this.'

'Might as well have a look round now we're here, though.' Usually Jonny was the nervous one, but now he grinned at Meg and punched her playfully on the shoulder. 'Or are you frightened?'

'It wasn't me who ran screaming from a man in a costume and paint,' Meg snapped.

Jonny considered this. 'I bet you would have done, though,' he decided.

'Why don't you and Flinch follow the path, while Jonny and I cut through between the stones?' Art said.

Meg sensed he was just finding an excuse to separate her and Jonny before they could argue any more. But it was not a real argument. Not like those her mum and dad had. Meg and Jonny would always be friends, even if they teased each other something rotten.

'All right,' Jonny said. 'So long as the girls are happy.'

He wasn't teasing now, Meg realised. He really was worried that Meg and Flinch might be frightened.

'We'll be fine,' she told him. 'Won't we?'

'Course we will,' Flinch agreed. 'We'll frighten any ghosts away for you, Jonny.'

'Meet you back here by the gate in a few minutes, then,' Art said before Jonny could respond to this.

It was a good thing that they were keeping to the path, Meg thought. She wondered how Art and

Jonny would find their way. The graveyard was not very big, but the mist was so thick now that they could be lost just yards from the path or the fence and never even realise. Several times, Meg strayed off the path, but she could immediately feel the difference between the hard gravel and the softer tufts of grass beneath her feet.

'What's that?' Flinch asked.

Meg was grateful that they were still holding hands. They could hardly even see each other.

Flinch was pointing at a vague dark shape to the side of the path. It looked like a shed or an outhouse. Cautiously, they stepped off the path to take a closer look. It was a small building made of old stone that was crumbling away at the corners and joins.

'A mausoleum, I think.'

'What's one of them?' Flinch asked.

'Like a tomb. A small building, like this, where a rich family buries its dead.'

'They dig up the ground inside?'

Meg wasn't really sure. 'There might be a crypt or something. A vault, with old stone coffins on shelves and stuff.'

'Spooky,' Flinch decided.

'Grotesque,' Meg agreed.

There was something unsettling about the old structure: the arched Gothic doorway with iron gates padlocked shut; a shallow, sloping lead roof above the stonework; a niche by the door with a weather-worn statue on a plinth watching them with sightless eyes. And above the doorway there were two gargoyles, their monstrous faces made even more bizarre by the way the rain had worn away their features. Meg shivered, and retraced her steps to the path.

Slightly further along, there was another large shape beside the path, but this one was not big enough to be a building.

'A tomb?' Flinch suggested.

'Could be.'

Again Meg led them carefully towards it, noting the route back to the path. 'Yes, you're right,' she said as they reached the shape. It was in effect a low stone box. Ivy was growing over it, and moss and lichen encrusted the sides. There was a raised stone step all round it, but the stone had worn away and several blocks were missing. The mist rolled across the heavy stone lid like steam from a kettle.

'Is there a dead body inside?' Flinch wanted to know.

'Maybe several. Sometimes they open up the grave again to put in a wife or husband or even children,' Meg said. 'After they've died, of course,' she added quickly.

Flinch was staring past Meg, still looking at the tomb as the older girl turned back towards the path. Her face was a pale mask of fear in the mist. Meg thought at first that it was the idea of death, of being sealed for ever in the icy-cold tomb. But fear was turning to terror and from behind came the hoarse grating sound of stone rubbing on stone.

Meg gripped Flinch's hand even more firmly and dragged her behind the nearest gravestone. Together they looked out from behind it, back at the tomb.

In time to see the heavy stone lid pivot and tilt. It slid away as if pushed up and off from the inside. Flinch gave a little squeak of fear and clapped her free hand over her mouth. Meg hugged her tight.

The lid had fallen away from the tomb and fog seemed to rise up like smoke from within. It was grey and dark, mixing with the lighter mist in the air outside. In the midst of the steaming fog, a figure appeared. It seemed to be rising up out of the tomb. Meg could see the face of the man as he looked round – deep-set eyes, bloodless lips, deathly pale skin.

The eyes fixed for a moment in Meg's direction and she ducked back behind the gravestone. Flinch was already curled up there, desperately trying to hide. Had they been seen? Meg did not dare to look back. If she did, she was sure she would see a pale, rotting figure stalking towards her out of the mist.

Sarah was happy to make a detour on the way home the next day. Arthur thought about suggesting they go to Northerton. But the idea of taking a girl to a graveyard seemed sort of weird. And she'd only want to stare at the crane and talk about Martin Michael. She already had the DVD of his latest TV series – he'd seen her showing it to her friends during morning break.

So instead Arthur suggested they go and see if

the Myton Museum still existed. To their surprise, it did. But it was in rather a run-down state. The whole place looked as if it ought to be some sort of exhibit itself. It had probably not changed very much from when Art and the others visited it all those years ago.

An elderly lady was sitting at a desk reading a battered paperback. She glanced up as they came in and then stared pointedly at a notice inviting visitors to make a contribution. Sarah had a couple of pounds, which she dropped into the wooden box. From the hollow sound they made, there was no other money in it.

The museum was basically one large, square room. Display cases were mounted on the walls and there were tables at intervals with exhibits on them. The glass of the cases was dusty. The labels, either handwritten or produced on an old type-writer a long time ago, were faded. Many were peeling away and some were so faint now they were all but impossible to read.

'It smells,' Sarah whispered as they made their way slowly round.

She was right. The whole place was old and musty.

'I don't think they get many visitors,' Arthur said.

Sarah gave a short laugh. 'I don't think they get *any* visitors.'

Perhaps the woman heard them, or perhaps she guessed what they were thinking. She looked up from her book and called across, 'We have applied for a lottery grant.' Her voice was as dry and old and dusty as the medieval shoe that Arthur was peering at in its case. 'Just a few thousand,' she went on. 'You'd think if they can waste hundreds of millions on the Dome they could spare us a few thousand, wouldn't you?' She was talking to her book now, her voice fading as she lost interest in her visitors.

Sarah was looking at the cases on the walls. She turned and waved to get Arthur's attention. 'There's some Roman stuff here,' she said.

He went to join her and together they looked into the case, at the jumble of coins and broken pottery. The labels here were just as faded. One of them Arthur fancied might say 'Donated by Brandon Lake and the Cannoniers'. He angled his head, trying to catch the light so that it shone on to the marks the pen had made on the card long ago. The ink had faded, leaving only an impression. Like the words on an old gravestone.

'That could be the coin they donated,' Arthur said. He wanted to believe it.

Sarah nodded, but said nothing.

'Probably aged more in the last seventy years than the two thousand before that,' Arthur told her.

'She'd know,' Sarah replied, nodding to the woman.

The woman seemed to sense the attention and again she glanced up at them. 'There's an interesting Roman sword at the end there, on the table,' she called across.

'Thank you,' Arthur called back.

He had seen enough and he could tell that Sarah was getting bored. But to be polite they walked along towards where the woman had gestured.

In the corner, at the end of the row of wall cabinets, was a low table. There was a clear plastic cover over it and inside was the sword. It was a typical Roman sword – short and broad, with a simple handle and guard. The blade was still bright, making it look newer than many of the more recent artefacts.

But the startling thing was not how well preserved it was but the fact that it was stuck through a small, ornate casket made of pale stone. The sword seemed to have been stabbed right through it.

'Must have taken a tremendous blow to do that,' Sarah said. 'I suppose it *is* stone.'

'It is.' They had not heard the woman join them. 'And the sword is so firmly thrust through that it is wedged in place. Can't be shifted. We did try to pull it out, but it wouldn't shift. My father always used to say that they must be left as they were found, and it seems that history agrees with him.'

As they were leaving, she handed Arthur a leaflet. It was slightly yellowed, curling up at the corner. From the design and the black and white photograph of the exhibition room, it looked as if it had been printed many years ago.

'Do come again.' The woman smiled thinly. 'And tell your friends about us. It's a shame that we're here and get so few visitors.'

Arthur and Sarah thanked her, promised to return and escaped into the late afternoon.

'You could taste the dust in the air,' Sarah complained. 'I bet they never clean.'

'The taste of history,' Arthur told her with a smile. He glanced at the leaflet before stuffing it into his pocket. 'The Myton Museum,' he read aloud. 'Proprietor and Curator: Anne Worthington (Miss).'

CHAPTER SIX

Meg forced herself to look. She edged as close as she could to the gravestone, steeled herself and peered round. Flinch was clutching her hand, not daring to look herself.

Through the swirling mist, Meg could see another pale figure emerging from the tomb – another man. But as a gust of wind blew the mist away in tatters, she could see that he looked so pale because he was wearing overalls that had once been white. Now they were stained and discoloured. The first man was waiting for him beside the tomb. He too was wearing overalls.

'Come on, mate,' he said gruffly. 'I don't want to be stuck here all day.'

Together they heaved the stone lid back over the top of the tomb. It seemed to be hinged and moved easily. Then they set off towards the path. Meg ducked back behind the gravestone, a finger on her lips to warn Flinch to keep quiet. Moments later the two men passed within a few feet of the girls. They were laughing at some joke, like two colleagues going off home at the end of their shift.

The girls gave the men time to get clear, then

followed back along the path towards the gate.

'Who were those men?' Flinch wanted to know. 'What were they doing in that tomb thing?'

'I don't know, Flinch. Maybe Art will have some idea.'

Meg was still trembling from the experience. She hoped they would not have to wait long for the boys – she wanted to leave and get home just as soon as she could.

Art and Jonny were already at the gate, waiting for them.

'You'll never guess what,' Jonny said excitedly as soon as they arrived. 'We had a good look round, but we couldn't really see much. Then, on the way back here, guess what?'

'You saw two men in overalls,' Meg said.

Jonny looked disappointed. Art laughed.

'They just appeared from nowhere,' Art said. 'Again. It's a mystery. I mean, where do they come from?'

'Out of the graves,' Flinch said.

She made it sound so matter of fact that Art laughed again.

'Don't be daft,' he said. 'These were real, living people.'

'I'm not being daft,' Flinch protested. 'Meg saw too. They came out of a big stone box, a tomb. Back there.' She turned and pointed into the mist. 'They did.'

'Really?' Jonny sounded dubious.

But Art's eyes were shining with eager anticipation. 'Show us,' he said. And Meg knew that she was not going to be leaving for home any time soon.

The tomb was the one that Art remembered from his previous exploration with Jonny. It looked normal enough, he thought, as tombs go. But both Meg and Flinch insisted that the lid could somehow be tilted open to allow a person to emerge like a Jack-in-the-box.

'There must be a hinge somewhere,' Jonny said. 'And a counterweight of some sort. This lid's far too heavy to shift otherwise.'

'The trick is to work out which way it moves,' Art said. 'Meg, how did it open? Can you remember?'

'I think this side tilted upwards and then it slid over towards where Jonny's standing. Isn't that right, Flinch?'

Flinch nodded. 'It made a scraping noise,' she said. 'It slid over a bit first, before it tilted up.'

Jonny was kneeling beside the tomb, running his fingers over the crumbling stone under the lip of the lid. 'I think this could be it,' he announced. 'Stand back. It's heavy.'

He pushed with both hands at the edge of the lid. From his expression, Art guessed he was surprised at how easily the lid moved.

They all recognised the scraping rasp of the stone as it shifted. Then the lid began to dip on one side and rise up on the other. Art and Jonny both caught hold of the rising edge and pulled it upwards, still dragging the stone lid across as they did. It rose and tilted and pivoted, and swung away to reveal the dark interior of the tomb.

'At least there's no one else inside,' Meg said, peering into the darkness.

'But why would they be hiding in a box?' Flinch asked.

'Because it isn't a box,' Art said. 'Look.'

He pointed into the tomb. As their eyes adjusted, they could see that there was a flight of stone steps leading down into the blackness.

'A cellar or something?' Meg wondered.

'Tunnel?' Jonny suggested. 'It can't be very long. It's heading towards the Thames.'

'Maybe it goes under the river,' Flinch said.

Jonny laughed. 'It would have to be quite deep.' But he stopped laughing as he considered. He looked back at the steps disappearing into the darkness. 'I suppose it's possible,' he admitted. 'We're quite low down here already, after all.'

'Well, wherever it goes, we need to find out,' Art decided.

'Do we?' Meg sounded dubious.

'Surely we should just get the police, or tell your dad or something,' Jonny said. He didn't sound too keen either.

'But we don't know what to tell them,' Flinch said. 'It's just a hole in the ground. We have to see what's down there, don't we, Art? Anyway, it'll be exciting.'

'It will if those men come back,' Jonny retorted. 'And what if there are more down there, waiting for us?'

'They don't know we're here,' Flinch said. She folded her arms, annoyed at Jonny's lack of enthusiasm.

'Right,' Art decided. 'I agree with Flinch. I

think we need to have some idea of what's going on before we can tell anyone else.' He shrugged. 'They might just be caretakers or gravediggers or something and this is where they store their tools and take their tea breaks.'

'You don't really think so, though,' Meg said.

'No, I don't. I still think there's something going on here that Bablock is keen to keep secret. But Flinch is right, we need a better idea of what it is, not just a vague suspicion.'

'So what do you suggest?'

'How about you and Jonny keep watch for us up here. Flinch and I will take a quick look – and I mean quick.'

'And how will you see anything down there?' Meg demanded. 'It's pitch dark.'

Art grinned and pulled his torch out of his coat pocket. He still had it with him from Monday night.

Jonny was frowning nervously. 'Are you sure it's safe?'

'If I was, I wouldn't need you and Meg to keep watch.'

'And if those men do come back?' Meg asked.

'Warn us if you can. Bang on the lid or something.'

Meg nodded. 'All right. We should close it up after you go, I suppose. You bang on the inside when you get back and we'll help you open it and get out.'

'And if I wait at the gate, I can run back and warn Meg if anyone comes,' Jonny said. 'Unless you think we should stick together?'

'I'll leave you two to decide what's best,' Art said quickly. 'Anyway, we won't be long. Just a quick look to see where the stairs lead. You coming, Flinch?'

The torch cast a pale yellow pool of light. The lid of the tomb slid easily back into place, cutting them off from the outside world. It was cold and damp inside the tomb, and Flinch shivered.

Art was examining the walls. They were made of brick. He poked at the lines of mortar between the bricks. 'I think this is fairly recent,' he said. 'There's no sign that it's been affected by the damp or age.'

'But where's it go?' Flinch wondered.

Art took her hand and together they made their way carefully down the steep stairs. They were damp and Flinch was careful not to slip. She didn't fancy tumbling into the blackness ahead of them. It seemed to go down for ever.

Eventually, the stairs stopped and they found themselves standing at the beginning of a tunnel. Art turned off the torch and they stood silent in the darkness. Except it was not dark. After a moment, Flinch realised she could still see Art – just the faint outline of his face close to hers.

'There's light,' she whispered.

He nodded and turned the torch back on. 'From down the tunnel somewhere.'

He shone the torch at the ground and they could see that the floor was made of stone slabs at the bottom of the stairs. As he moved the torch along, the slabs stopped and the floor was dull, grey concrete.

'That looks rather older,' Art said.

He led Flinch a short way along the tunnel, then stopped to examine the walls. They arched over Flinch's head in a semicircle, like a railway tunnel. The ceiling must be twenty feet or more above her, she realised. The walls were still made of brick, but when Art prodded at them with his finger, a trickle of dry mortar flaked away.

'I think this tunnel has been here for a while,' he went on.

'But you said the stairs were new.'

'Yes. A new way to get to a tunnel that's been closed off and abandoned.'

'But what's it for? It's huge.'

They headed towards the light. After a few yards, Art turned off the torch. 'Don't want to attract attention,' he said quietly. 'If there's light, there are probably people. And you were right.'

'What about?' Flinch whispered back.

By way of answer, Art turned the torch back on. He shone it at the wall beside them. An enormous door made of heavy metal was opened back against the wall. It was curved to fit the shape of the tunnel. Or rather, half the tunnel, because on the opposite wall was another door – a mirror image. And above them, running round the inside of the tunnel, was a metal strip. Another strip was set into the concrete floor.

'Flood gates,' Art said. 'If there is a leak, they close the gates. There may be more at intervals all through the tunnel. So they can seal off any section if there's a danger of flooding, or for repairs or whatever.' He pointed to a metal wheel standing proud of the wall slightly further along. 'Look, there's the closing mechanism. And if the tunnel floods, the weight of the water will simply force the gates shut anyway.'

Flinch had noticed something else. Two more strips of metal set into the floor, starting just before the gates and running the length of the tunnel as far as she could see.

'What's that? They look like railway lines.'

'Tramlines,' Art realised. 'This must be a tram tunnel. Or was going to be. Dad told me once they were going to put tunnels under the Thames about thirty years ago so the trams didn't have to use the bridges. He said they abandoned the idea. But maybe they built this tunnel before they changed their minds.'

'Why didn't they fill it in?'

'Why bother? They probably just blocked up the ends and forgot about it.' He turned the torch off again. 'Though it seems someone didn't forget.'

A few yards further on, they stopped again.

'Can you hear that?' Art said quietly.

Flinch nodded. She had not noticed it until now, but the tunnel seemed to be breathing.

Heavy, rhythmic sounds whispering in the dim light. Louder now – metallic and mechanical. It could almost be one of the trams that the tunnel had been built for, rumbling towards them along the rusty rails.

'We're certainly not alone,' Art said.

They had decided on a compromise. Jonny didn't want to be on his own at the gate and Meg didn't want to be on her own at the tomb. Neither of them would admit this to the other, but they had come to the agreement that it would be sensible if they stayed together. And since they needed to be within earshot of the tomb for when Art and Flinch returned, and they wanted to keep watch for anyone arriving at the graveyard, they found themselves halfway between the tomb and the gate.

Which put them outside the crumbling mausoleum. From here, Jonny was confident he would have ample time to run to the tomb and sound a warning if anyone came. And Meg was sure she would hear if Art and Flinch hammered on the inside of the lid for help.

It had started to rain, so they were pressed into the doorway of the small stone building, up against the rusty metal gates. The rain had washed the mist away and they could now see both the tomb and the gate clearly. Because it was summer, Meg wasn't worried about being out late, though she could have done with some more typical summer weather.

Jonny was bored, fiddling with the chain that held the gates closed. Meg told him to leave it alone, but he seemed fascinated.

'The chain's old,' he said, 'but the padlock's quite new.'

'So, the old one broke or something. Just leave it.'

But Jonny was intrigued now. 'It's not very good,' he said. 'I reckon I could open this easily.' He pulled out his penknife and set to work.

'You're supposed to be keeping a lookout,' Meg said.

'I am keeping a lookout.'

'No, you're not.'

'There's nothing to see.'

'How do you know? You're fiddling with that padlock.'

Jonny sighed and closed his knife. 'Art said they'd be straight back.'

'They haven't been gone that long.'

'I wonder what they've found,' Jonny said.

The rain was falling more heavily and the wind was angling it in at them in the doorway.

'Whatever it is, I hope they *are* back soon,' Meg said. 'I'm getting soaked.'

The noise grew steadily louder as they moved further along the tunnel. Art estimated they must have been well under the Thames by the time the tunnel divided. The largest, main tunnel continued on, curving away to the left. Two smaller tunnels now ran parallel, with occasional archways linking them back to the main one. Service tunnels perhaps, Art thought – carrying power cables and gas and water pipes.

There were electric lamps at intervals on the tunnel walls. They seemed more modern than the tunnel itself – presumably installed by whoever was now using the underground facility. Part of the noise they could hear might be a generator. Once they were closer, it was obvious that there were several machines at least, all working slightly out of time and at different pitches.

'I think we should stick to the side tunnels,' Art told Flinch.

He had to speak at normal volume to be heard above the noise. There was a smell too, he realised. Not just the damp, musty smell of the tunnel itself but an oily, slightly acrid smell that caught in his throat.

Soon the lamps were closer together and it became much easier to see. As well as the noise of machinery they could hear people shouting to each other. Finally, as they reached another archway that gave back on to the main tunnel, they saw what was happening.

There must have been about twenty men in all, dressed in similar white overalls. The exception was a man in a suit standing by one of the machines.

'That's Mr Bablock,' Flinch told Art.

The machines were arranged at intervals along the tunnel floor – large, heavy metal beasts. Flywheels whirred and pistons hissed. Trays rose and fell rhythmically, and Art realised what he was looking at.

'It's a printing works,' he told Flinch.

'What are they printing?'

But something else had caught Art's attention now. Up beside the lamp above their heads a wire was looping down. He thought at first it was attached to the light, but now he saw that it was actually part of a small box beside the lamp. He had noticed similar boxes by some of the other lamps along the way – dull, grey, gunmetal. This one was exactly like those, except that the cover had fallen open and he could see what was inside. A red cylinder, about eight inches long, with a pair of wires attached to the end. Stencilled in heavy block letters of black ink on the side of the cylinder were two words: DANGER: EXPLOSIVE.

'Flinch,' Art said quietly, unable to take his eyes off the writing.

There was no answer. He forced himself to look away.

Flinch had gone.

He felt panic welling up inside him and looked round desperately. He saw her at last, standing close to the pillar that formed the side of the next archway. Art ran to join her, dashing quickly across the closer archway, hoping he would not be spotted.

'What are you doing?' he hissed, barely loud

enough for her to hear him above the sound of the machine that was operating just through the archway.

In reply, Flinch nodded at the machine. From where they were standing, beside the pillar, they were hidden from the view of the men in the tunnel. But they had a clear sight of what the machine was printing. Beside it another machine of a slightly different design was stamping out small pieces of metal that dropped through to collect in a large wire tray beneath it. Art looked from one tray to the other, from paper to metal.

From crisp new five-pound notes to shining new half-crowns.

'It's money,' Flinch said. 'They're making money.'

'The counterfeiters,' Art said. 'And they've got this whole placed rigged to blow up if they're found. So they can flood the tunnel and destroy the evidence.'

He turned from Flinch to look back at the machines as they churned out coin after coin, banknote after banknote. Standing beside another of the machines, in the middle of the tunnel, the lean figure of Bablock was inspecting one of the notes, smiling and nodding with satisfaction. Then the smile froze and the note fluttered to the floor. He was staring down at the ground, frowning.

And only then did Art realise that the lamp on the wall behind them was casting their shadows huge and dark across the tunnel floor. Their elongated silhouettes lay in profile at Bablock's feet.

Five days into the stunt and the media frenzy had faded to a mild interest. Even Sarah had stopped talking about Martin Michael and how brave he was. But all that changed in the evening.

Arthur saw it on the news when he got back from school. He missed the opening explanation, because Dad was telling him how ridiculous the whole thing was and that Michael should have more sense and what was the youth of today coming to and it was only a marketing stunt. As if Arthur needed telling.

'So what's happened?' Arthur wanted to know.

Dad shrugged. 'Maybe he's sprung a leak.'

They both laughed.

Then the picture cut from the reporter on the Embankment to the view from one of the cameras mounted on the glass cage under the Thames. It showed Michael, looking the worse for wear – his eyes deep-set and dark, his face covered with stubble. It didn't help that the bright light built into the lid of the tank made him look so pale and waxen.

'Then at just before four-thirty this afternoon, after five days of what I can only describe as inactivity, *this* happened.'

Arthur and his dad both leaned closer. The picture was not very clear – grainy and colour-faded. As they watched Michael yawned and looked out of the side of the tank. Then he seemed to stiffen suddenly, before pushing himself back from the side. Soon he had his back pressed against the opposite wall, staring out into the water. The camera was angled at Michael, so they could not see what he was looking at. But they could hear him – his voice filtered through the microphones and cables, tinny but recognisable. And frightened.

'Neil – Neil, can you hear me? Neil, there's

something out there. I can see it. Coming towards the tank. I thought it was a fish or something, but . . .'

Then Michael gave a cry of fear and turned away, burying his face against the glass.

The picture cut again – to an even grainier image. The view out of the tank, showing whatever Michael had seen. Over this, another voice – Neil, urgent and anxious.

'Martin, Martin, are you all right? What's going on? Do you want to come up? I can see the image through the west side of the tank. I don't see . . . *What's that?!*'

Arthur could see it too. Even though he was only watching on a television screen, he gave a gasp and felt his heart miss a beat.

A shape was solidifying out of the murky blackness. Pressing against the side of the tank. A dark silhouette, clamped suddenly to the glass, deep under the Thames.

A hand.

CHAPTER SEVEN

Quickly, Art took hold of Flinch by the shoulders and pulled her back behind the pillar.

'Our shadows,' he said. 'He saw our shadows.'

Flinch nodded her understanding and Art relaxed, letting go of her. Immediately she ran back to the previous archway and looked out. Art hurried to join her. Bablock was still staring down at the floor, though of course the silhouetted shapes of Art and Flinch had gone. Puzzled, Bablock looked across to where Art and Flinch had been. Art could see the man frowning as he thought through the possibilities. He stooped to retrieve the fake banknote he had dropped, then walked slowly over towards where Art and Flinch had been.

'He'll see us,' Flinch said.

She was right. As soon as Bablock reached the archway, he would be able to see them further along the side tunnel, caught full in the light from the back wall. They could not hide behind the arch or they would be in full view of the men in the main tunnel. There was only one chance.

'Run!' Art said.

They ran, hand in hand, as fast as they could. It didn't matter that their feet slapped noisily on the concrete floor, as the sound was masked by the printing and pressing machines. But they had to reach the next archway – beyond the area where the men were working – before Bablock turned the corner and saw them.

Gasping for breath, they all but fell into the shelter of the archway, pressing themselves against the cold brick wall. Art dared not look back. Bablock would be looking round, wondering what had cast such peculiar shadows. Perhaps he had seen them. Perhaps even now he was walking down the tunnel towards where they were hiding – calling for his men to follow. Was he about to appear in the archway and confront them? Art felt cold at the thought, though the air was heavy with the heat from the machinery.

It was Flinch who dared to look back first. Art was still pressed into the wall, wondering how long to wait before checking. But Flinch stuck her head out into the side corridor, just for a split second. Then she whipped it back again.

'Is he there?' Art asked urgently, prepared to run again. 'Is he coming?'

'Didn't see anyone,' Flinch told him. 'Hang on.' She stuck her head out again. 'No, I think he's gone.'

The noise of the machinery was quieter here, further down the tunnel. Which was how Art was able to hear Bablock's voice. It sounded as if he was approaching – not from the side tunnel, but walking along the main tunnel.

'. . . And I've had enough of people helping themselves,' he was saying. 'I want everyone searched when they go off shift. Make sure they know that, Galman. Now that we've dealt with Quainton and retrieved what he found, all eyes should be on Stepney. Let's keep it that way.'

'Yes, Mr Bablock,' a quieter, deferential voice replied. 'We, er, we still need to decide what to do with the rest of the, er, the other material.' The voice was definitely getting closer.

'Then let's sort that out now. Decide what to move and what to keep here out of the way.'

'Come on,' Art mouthed to Flinch.

If they didn't move now, Bablock and whoever was with him would get ahead of them, cutting off their escape. There was no guarantee that the other end of the tunnel was open, or even that it had ever been finished. They would have to leave the way they had come in. Art wanted to be out before Bablock reached the tomb himself, and they had to be far enough ahead by the time the tunnels joined into one again so that Bablock wouldn't see them. At least the lighting was more subdued further along.

Together they ran down the side corridor as fast as they could. When they reached the junction, Art and Flinch slowed to a halt. Art leaned out to look back along the main corridor. There was no sign yet of Bablock.

'Quick!' he urged Flinch.

And they were off again, running for all they were worth through the thickening blackness. Because Art did not dare turn on his torch, for fear that Bablock would see it, they were soon running in complete darkness.

After a while, they slowed to a brisk walk. Art held on to Flinch with one hand, while with the other he reached out ahead, worried they might hit the end of the tunnel.

But it was not the end wall that was his

undoing. His foot caught on the bottom step of the stairs up to the entrance hidden in the tomb and he sprawled forward, pulling Flinch with him.

'Sorry, are you all right?'

Art had barked his knee on the corner of the step and it hurt like heck. He rubbed at it to dull the pain. Flinch was just visible in the gloom close by. Her dark silhouette was nodding, so he knew she was fine.

'I hope Jonny and Meg are still there,' Flinch said.

Art risked the torch so they could find their way up without further mishap. Once at the top of the steps, he hammered on the low ceiling above him which he knew was really the lid of the tomb. He shone the torch all round, but could see no opening mechanism – no lever or pulley or handhold. The mechanism must be built into the wall itself. Art's fist beat a dull rhythm on the stone, echoing slightly in the stairwell.

But from outside, there was no sound of a reply.

The rain was hammering down now. Jonny and Meg were scrunched into the shelter of the doorway of the mausoleum. The rain was running off the roof and cascading down in front of them in a solid sheet.

'Done it,' Jonny proclaimed with excitement.

'What?' Meg was glumly watching the rain.

Jonny proudly showed her the padlock he had removed from the chain holding the gates shut. He pushed the gates open enough to give them more room.

But Meg was still not impressed. 'We can't stay here.'

'Why not?' Jonny stared at her in astonishment. 'I'm not going out *there*,' he said, nodding at the water pouring down in front of them.

The sky was almost black with cloud – it seemed more like night-time than late afternoon. A flash of summer lightning illuminated the waterfall from the top of the door.

'And what if Art and Flinch need our help?'

Jonny frowned. 'Can't we go *then*? Surely there's no need to go now.'

'Except we won't know, will we? We can't see the tomb from inside here and we won't hear if they call for help. Not above all that.'

As if to emphasise Meg's point, there was a rumble of thunder. Jonny took an instinctive step backwards, into the mausoleum. His feet caught on the uneven flagstones of the floor and he tumbled over with a cry.

Meg went to help as more lightning stabbed through the darkness. For a moment the inside of the mausoleum was lit up and Meg could see that there were several doors from the main room, leading, she assumed, into the family vaults. Certainly there seemed to be no stone caskets or gravestones in this room. Just Jonny lying on the ground and making no effort to get up.

'Did you see it?' he gasped.

'The lightning?' Meg reached down and took his hand, pulling him to his feet.

'No, through there.'

Meg could barely make out where Jonny was pointing.

'Come on.'

'What? Where?' Meg pulled back, towards the entrance.

But Jonny still had hold of her hand and he was dragging her further inside, towards one of the dimly visible doorways.

'It was like a glow. Just for a moment. From through here.'

Meg almost collided with the side of the doorway. 'Careful,' she warned.

They stopped on the threshold of the room beyond, neither wanting to take the first step inside, neither able to see in the gloom.

Then the lightning flashed again and they both gasped in unison as they saw what lay inside.

'We'd better tell Art,' Jonny said.

'We'd better find him,' Meg agreed.

They made their way carefully back to the entranceway. Jonny pulled the gates shut and pushed the padlock through the two ends of the chain to hold them together. But he left the padlock open.

With a deep breath and a glance at each other, they plunged out into the darkness and the rain. But even through the storm, they could see a light bobbing its way along the pavement outside the graveyard.

'They might just be going past,' Jonny said. He had to talk loudly to be heard above the sound of the rain splattering on the gravel path, the grass, the gravestones, the road, the leaded roof of the mausoleum.

'Out for a nice walk?' Meg countered. 'Just happened to take a torch with him in the middle of the afternoon? I don't think so. Come on.'

As the light paused at the gate, Meg and Jonny ran, drenched, for the tomb.

There was a sound from outside now. But it was not the heavy thumping that Art expected in reply to his own hammering on the unyielding stone. It was a lighter, rhythmic tap-tapping, like someone drumming their fingers or scattering gravel.

Flinch was at the bottom of the stone staircase. She ran up to join Art, her pale face seeming washed out in the glow of the torch.

'They're coming,' she whispered. 'Bablock and that other man. I can see their torches along the tunnel.'

'Come on, Jonny!' Art hissed in frustration. He banged as hard as he could on the heavy lid covering the top of the tomb. 'Come on!'

There were voices now, from the bottom of the stairs.

Flinch was pushing at the lid. Art switched off

the torch. 'Sorry, Flinch,' he murmured. He could not tell if she heard. Any moment now, Bablock and the other man – Galman – would start up the stairs, and would find them trapped at the top.

'We'll decide now,' Bablock's words carried easily to Art and Flinch. Two beams of torchlight played over the lower steps. 'Then it's done.'

'Of course, Mr Bablock.'

One of the torches swung upwards. Almost reached Art. Then it swung down again.

'Open the doorway, Galman.'

'Of course, Mr Bablock.'

Art fumbled for Flinch's hand. Below them, Galman was shining his torch along the wall at the bottom of the steps. It picked out a dark shadow, something jutting from the wall that neither Art nor Flinch had noticed – a lever.

'Of course,' Art murmured, just loud enough for Flinch to hear. 'They open it from down there.' He gripped her hand. 'Get ready to squeeze out, soon as you can. I'll be right behind you.'

The man with the torch had started along the gravel path. Jonny could see his silhouette – barely recognisable as that of a man, his collar was turned up so high and his hat pulled down so low. It resembled a drawing in charcoal. The rain shone like lines of silver in the torchlight.

'He'll see us in a minute,' Meg said. 'We won't have time to get the lid open.'

'We won't need to,' Jonny told her as they arrived beside the tomb. He pointed. The lid was already sliding slowly open, grating back and sideways as it started to tilt.

Meg gasped as a pale hand emerged into the rain. It felt round the top of the tomb, then an arm followed. As soon as the opening was wide enough – in fact, well before it looked anything like wide enough – Flinch's unmistakable form squeezed through and tumbled to the muddy ground. Meg ran to help her up.

Jonny was peering into the darkness as the lid continued to open. Another hand was groping upwards. Somewhere down below a light was shining – was swinging up towards Art's shadowy form. Jonny grabbed his friend's arm and yanked him out of the opening.

Art stumbled as he landed beside Jonny. They held on to each other for a moment to keep from slipping, grinning in the near-darkness.

Then a puddle light shone across the side of the tomb, reminding Jonny of the man who was approaching. He pulled Art away and they ducked behind a gravestone. Jonny was not surprised to find Meg already there. Flinch was with her, muddy and bedraggled. She looked accusingly at Jonny.

'It's raining,' Flinch said.

The man had now arrived at the tomb and he was calling down into the blackness, though his words were lost in the hammering of the rain.

'What did you find?' Meg wanted to know.

'Tunnels,' Flinch told her. 'And the forgers.'

'Let's get somewhere dry and we can talk,' Art said quietly.

'The mausoleum,' Jonny told him. 'We've got something to show you there.'

They hurried, wet and cold, through the rain to the mausoleum. Jonny slipped the unlocked padlock from the chain and swung open the gates. He led them into the darkened interior and Art switched on his torch.

Meg closed the gates and pulled the chain back into place. She could not reach far enough through the ironwork to reposition the padlock, so she simply hooked it through a loop at one end of the chain and then draped the chain through the ornate metal curls that made up the gate.

'Through here,' Jonny told them, leading the way.

He stepped aside to allow Art and Flinch to go first. Jonny and Meg exchanged glances, smiling as they heard the gasps of astonishment. Flinch stepped back out of the small chamber, her eyes gleaming in the dim light.

'Treasure!' she said.

Art was shining the torch over the glittering pile. Ornamental armour, helmets and breast-plates gleamed, while multi-faceted jewels reflected the light. An ornate casket of pale stone stood lopsided on a small heap of coins like the one Albert Norris had produced.

'Must be a fortune here,' Meg said. 'Don't you think, Art?'

'Certainly to a historian. Don't know how valuable those stones and jewels really are. They may be just glass and stuff.'

'But what's it doing here?' Flinch said. 'Someone would have found it.'

'Someone has found it,' Jonny told her. 'And

put it here to keep it safe and hidden. Except that man Quainton got in somehow. I bet that's why there's a new padlock,' he realised.

'Sheltering from the rain, maybe,' Meg said.

'Bablock must have found it when he was digging down to the tunnel,' Art said. 'And then when the rumours started, they shifted some of it to Stepney to divert attention. They wouldn't want people digging about round here.' He had been shining the torch back and forth over the treasure. Now it froze. 'Wait a minute. Flinch, you remember what Bablock was saying?'

'How much to keep and how much to move.' Flinch nodded. 'He meant the treasure.'

'Yes. He said he was going to have a look and decide, remember?' Art turned, the torch now illuminating his friends, his voice a hoarse whisper. 'He's coming here.'

Even as Art spoke, the sound of the chain jangling and clanging came from outside.

'Funny,' a gruff voice said. 'Wasn't properly locked.'

'More slacking and carelessness,' Bablock's voice replied.

'This way,' Jonny hissed. 'Quick!'

They darted out of the room and immediately through an adjacent doorway. The room they were now in was probably very similar, but it was dark so it was impossible to tell. A thin strip of a window at the far side of the room let in meagre illumination and the sound of the rain.

Jonny and Art ushered Meg and Flinch into the room. The two boys stood close to the doorway, watching as the light from the men's torches crossed the floor. As Jonny had guessed, all three men went into the next room – the one they had themselves just left.

'Narrow squeak,' Jonny whispered.

Art nodded. 'Let's have a look and see what they're up to.'

Jonny was not at all sure this was a good idea. But he followed Art into the main area of the mausoleum and together they stood in the shadow of the next doorway. They peered carefully round the door frame.

Inside, two of the men were shining their torches over the little heap of treasure. The third, Bablock, had stooped down and was examining it. He pushed coins aside, lifted away a breastplate, examined a helmet . . .

'There's nothing much left now,' he announced. 'But it's probably best not to leave it around. Too much of a temptation for some.'

'There's a lot of activity at the other site,' the man with the gruff voice said. He still had his collar turned right up. 'Could be tricky moving it there.'

'We could bury it,' the other, smaller man suggested.

'And have someone go and dig it up again?' gruff-voice said scathingly.

'I didn't mean here.'

Bablock had picked up the stone casket. 'We'll leave it here for now,' he decided. 'But cover it up with a tarpaulin or something, in case any other idiot wanders in. And, Marsden, make sure everyone knows what will happen to anyone who tries to help himself.'

'Right, Mr Bablock,' gruff-voice said.

The casket was obviously heavy. Bablock held it in both hands, examining each side carefully in the light from the torches.

'This is an interesting piece,' he observed. He ran a finger down one side, tracing a curved line across the stone. 'Cracked. A pity.'

'George Lawrence hit it with his spade,' the smaller man said. 'Chipped a bit off. It's locked solid, though. Doesn't seem any way of opening it. But I don't think there's anything inside. It's heavy because it's stone, that's all.'

Bablock had pulled out a pocket knife. He pushed the blade into the hairline crack. 'Wasn't made to be opened, that's for sure,' he said quietly. 'It's sealed up tight. Ornamental, perhaps.' His eyes were shining in the torchlight – pale and grey. He leaned closer to the casket, hunched over it as he tried to force the knife further in, head down so his face was hidden. He seemed to freeze, just for a moment. Then abruptly, he pulled the knife out, closed the blade and put it away. 'We'll take this with us,' he announced. His voice seemed to echo slightly in the small room. It was deeper than it had been, slightly husky.

When Bablock straightened up and turned towards the door, Jonny saw that the centres of the man's eyes were now as black as the night, as if his pupils were enormously enlarged. But then Art was pulling him away, back into the next room, before Bablock and the others noticed them.

'His eyes!' Jonny hissed. 'Did you see his eyes?'

'Yes,' Art whispered back.

But there was no time for them to say anything more. Bablock and his two men walked briskly past the doorway, Bablock carrying the stone casket. There was the sound of the gate clanging shut. The rattle of the chain. Then just the spattering of the rain against the sill of the tiny window at the back of the room.

'His eyes,' Jonny said at once. 'They just went black. You saw, didn't you, Art?'

'I saw something. Trick of the light, maybe.'

'He was right in front of the torch.'

'What are you two babbling about?' Meg demanded.

Art turned his torch back on to reveal Meg standing with her arms folded, framed by the narrow arched top of the window. She was frowning. 'Where's Flinch?'

Flinch was behind them, standing in the doorway. 'They've locked the gates.'

'That's all right,' Meg told her. 'Jonny can pick the padlock.'

But Flinch shook her head. 'I don't think he

can. Even I can't get my hand through far enough to reach it.' Her eyes were wide, her hair plastered to her pale face. 'We're locked in.'

'Maybe we can reach it with a stick or something. Pull the padlock closer,' Art suggested. 'Let's see.'

But it was no use. The padlock was hanging low on the chain. Higher up the gate, the ironwork was open enough for Flinch to get her arm through. But lower down, near the padlock, the pattern was more closely knit and she could barely get her fingers through.

'At least those men have gone,' Meg said.

'Have they?' Flinch pointed across the rain-swept graveyard outside. 'Then who's that?'

There was a figure, standing in the darkness. It had not been there a moment ago, Jonny was sure. The shape was becoming more substantial, as if it was fading into existence even as he watched.

'There's another one,' Art said quietly.

'And another,' Meg said.

They were all pointing in different directions now. And across the graveyard, unaffected by the driving rain, the vague shadowy forms of figures faded into definition and gained substance.

The rain continued to fall around them, turning the ground to mud. Spattering through the figures as if they were not there. Fully armoured Roman soldiers, standing stiffly to attention among the gravestones.

Of course, Sarah would talk about nothing else the next day after school.

'He was so brave. I'd have freaked out.'

'He did freak out,' Arthur told her.

She ignored him.

'I mean, it looked *so* like a hand, didn't it? I know they're saying it was just a clump of weed or something and a trick of the light, the shadows. But he didn't know that any more than we did.'

'Probably a publicity stunt. Frogman with a funny glove. When's he come out anyway? When's it all finish?' Arthur asked, deciding there was no way she would let him change the subject. 'Tomorrow, isn't it?'

'Yeah. Five o'clock. I'm going to tape it.'

'I thought I'd go and see Grandad,' Arthur said.

He at least wouldn't be bothered by watching Martin Michael hauled out of the river to a hero's welcome.

'I'll come with you,' Sarah said. 'We can watch it together there. Your grandad'll be interested, and he's got a video, hasn't he?'

Arthur didn't answer.

'Where are we going?' Sarah asked.

Arthur had just been walking. He hadn't really thought where they were going. Or he had assumed that Sarah knew. He slowed and looked round, realising where they were.

'We're going to the cemetery at Northerton,' he said.

'Why? Checking up on the Romans again?'

'Could be,' Arthur admitted. 'But there's a good view of the crane and everything too.'

She frowned and shook her head. 'What crane?'

'The one ready to haul your mate Martin Michael out of the river next time a bit of weed floats up and scares him.'

Again the graveyard was coated with a faint mist from the river, but nothing like as much as there had been the last time. Sarah walked slowly along the path.

'It's just a cemetery,' she said. 'Doesn't look like it's used any more. Dead people.' She pulled a face. 'Great.'

'The mausoleum's just along here,' Arthur said.

She had read through the final case in the book just as Arthur had. She knew what had happened here, though it was hard to reconcile the place in harsh daylight with Art's descriptions of that night back in 1937.

They stood in front of the small building. Sarah pulled at the chain. Although it was old and rusty, it seemed firm enough.

'The tomb must be further on,' she said, letting the padlock drop. 'I wonder if it still opens up.'

'Let's see.'

He turned to go, and found that there was someone else with them, standing a short way down the path. A man.

It was the man who had greeted him by name the other day. The mist was getting thicker now, swirling round the figure like a shroud, making him seem indistinct.

'He's back,' Arthur said quietly. 'That man.'

'What man?' Sarah turned to look.

'I told you about him, remember?' Arthur said.

He took a few paces forward and said more loudly, 'Hello again.'

The man nodded, his features shadowed. 'Arthur Drake.'

'How do you know who I am?' There was no answer, so Arthur went on, 'The policeman said he'd never seen you before, but you told me you live here. You're not from round here, though, are you?'

'No,' the man admitted. 'This is not my homeland. But I have been here for ... many years. Waiting to wield again the sword of truth. Over the years I have picked up your language.' He seemed amused by this.

'You speak it very well,' Arthur assured him. 'Doesn't he?' He turned to Sarah.

She was staring into the mist, frowning, her mouth open in surprise. 'What are you doing?' she said, her voice catching slightly as if she was frightened.

'Just talking.'

'But ... who are you talking to?' She pointed straight at the figure in the mist. 'There's no one there. Just the mist.'

Arthur gaped. There was certainly someone there. Why couldn't Sarah see him?

The man was nodding again. 'Only you can see me, Arthur,' he said quietly. 'I've been waiting for *you*.'

Arthur laughed at that. 'Don't be daft.'

'It's just the mist,' Sarah retorted, assuming he was talking to her. 'You're the one being daft.' She punched him on the arm. 'Stop mucking about. You really had me going then. I should know better by now. Come on. Let's look at this tomb.'

Sarah set off down the path, into – and through – the patch of mist where the man had been standing only moments ago. The mist drifted away as she passed. There was no one else there.

At the point where the man had been standing, Sarah paused and turned back to face Arthur. 'You coming or what?' She laughed at his expression. 'I dunno. You're trying to spook me, but it's you who looks like he's seen a ghost.'

CHAPTER EIGHT

The figures of the Roman soldiers were now solid enough to be real. The rain was running down their helmets and breastplates. Still they stood stiffly to attention – all silent and motionless, all identical.

Except, Art realised, for one. He had a red plume on his helmet that marked him out, presumably, as the leader. As Art and the others watched, helpless, from behind the locked gates of the mausoleum, this soldier stepped out of the shadows. He turned to survey his fellows, nodding grimly as he also took in his surroundings.

'We have to get out of here,' Jonny said nervously.

'Thank you,' Meg told him. 'I think we know that.'

'Or maybe we should just hide here,' Jonny added as he thought about it. 'Maybe they'll go away.'

'And maybe not,' Meg whispered.

Flinch was again scrabbling for the padlock, still unable to reach. Art's mind was racing. There was something at the back of his memory. Something he had seen recently – the rain, angling down, framed by . . . a window.

'Flinch, there's a window back in that little room. It's too narrow for any of us to get through but you might manage.'

She nodded quickly.

'Wait.' Jonny gave her his penknife, so she could pick the padlock.

'You could have handed that to her through the gate,' Meg said as Flinch turned to go.

Jonny waited till she was out of earshot before he replied. Art was following, ready to help Flinch up to the window. But he caught Jonny's words as he left.

'She might need to defend herself before she gets back to the gate.'

He was right, of course, Art realised. They had no way of knowing what the soldiers intended. He hoped, really hoped, they were just play-acting, like the soldier at Sydenham had been. But he remembered how they had seemed to fade into existence, how the rain had splashed through them. If they were genuine Romans who had somehow found themselves brought forward to the 1930s, then who knew what they might do in their confusion and surprise and fear.

His torch picked out the stone frame of the window. It was even narrower than he remembered, though Flinch seemed undeterred.

'Do you think the soldiers are friendly?' she asked as Art made a cradle out of his hands.

She stepped into it and he heaved her up to the window.

'I don't know,' he admitted. 'Best be wary of them.'

'Wary?'

She stood on the narrow sill, turned sideways and started to wriggle herself through. Art could hear the click as she dislocated her shoulder in order to manoeuvre it through the narrow opening.

'Be careful. Straight to the front, and then Jonny can tell you how to pick the lock and let us out.'

He watched, amazed as ever at how Flinch was able to wriggle herself through such a tiny space. She grinned back at him.

'See you in a minute,' Flinch said. And with that, she was through the window and disappearing into the rain-swept night.

Running to the gate, the torchlight dancing as he moved, Art was back before Flinch got there. But only just. Her grinning face appeared at the gates in moments. She waved Jonny's penknife and set to work with its thin blade.

'Just sort of jiggle it,' Jonny said. 'When you feel resistance, push and see if you can get it to open.'

It took a few minutes, with Flinch becoming more and more frustrated while Jonny became increasingly agitated. Meg and Art each tried to calm the two of them down. Only when Flinch gave a shriek of triumph and the padlock clattered to the floor did Art see that the nearest of the Roman soldiers was watching with interest.

It was the leader, the one with the scarlet plume on his helmet. As Art and the others crowded out of the gate and stood on the edge of the rain, the soldier stepped towards them. His hand, Art noticed, was on the hilt of the short sword he wore at his side.

The other soldiers were turning to watch, Art counted seven of them. Each and every one had his hand on his sword, waiting for the leader's cue to action.

Then the leader spoke. His voice was low and

gravelly. '*Pax vobiscum*,' he said.

'What?' Art shook his head. 'I don't understand,' he told the soldier. He gestured to the other soldiers, all watching keenly. 'Who are you? Where did you come from?' Instinctively he was speaking loudly, hoping this would help.

But the soldier shook his head. The rain was running down his breastplate in narrow rivers. '*Pulvis et umbra sumus.*'

'What's he saying?' Flinch demanded, pushing past Meg so she was standing next to Art in front of the tall soldier.

She smiled at the man and, to everyone else's surprise, he smiled back. His hand left his sword and he patted her gently on the head.

'*Nescio quid dicas*,' the soldier said.

'He's speaking in Latin,' Art realised. 'It's what the ancient Romans spoke.'

'But we don't,' Flinch pointed out. 'Are they really from olden times, then?'

'Two thousand years ago,' Jonny told her. 'More or less.'

The soldier watched them as they spoke, still shaking his head. '*Quod incepimus conficiemus*,' he said quietly, and turned away.

'I know someone who speaks Latin,' Meg said as they watched the soldier march back to his men.

'Really?' Jonny was impressed.

'So do you,' she told him. 'Mr Worthington.'

Art nodded. 'Yes, I bet he does. Or if not, he'll know someone who can help. Still, at least they don't seem to mean us any harm.'

'And they seem happy enough to talk,' Meg pointed out. 'Or this one does. It's just we don't understand him.'

'I expect Worthington's still in Stepney,' Art was thinking out loud. 'At the fake site.'

'I don't think we'll persuade these soldiers to leave their posts,' Jonny said. 'They're here for a reason. That man seems pretty determined. Anyway, we don't want Roman soldiers running round London, whether they're real or not.'

They all turned to look at the leader, who was once more standing to attention beside one of the gravestones. He had all but disappeared into the shadows. Watching and waiting – but for what?

'We could ask Mr Worthington to come here,' Flinch suggested.

'Oh, yes,' Jonny said sarcastically. 'Excuse

174

me, Mr Worthington, but we've found where the real treasure is and it's being guarded by the pretty substantial ghosts of Roman soldiers who will only speak to us in Latin. Could you come and translate for us, please?'

Flinch stared back at him. 'Are they really guarding the treasure?'

'I don't know,' Art told her. He turned to Jonny and clapped him on the shoulder. 'Well, since you have the speech down pat and he knows you better than any of us, I think you're the man for the job.'

'What?' Jonny's eyes widened. He shook his head, sending water dripping from his wet hair. 'Me?'

'Be as quick as you can,' Meg said.

The rain faded to a merciful drizzle as Jonny made his way to Stepney. He had gambled that Mr Worthington was up at the site where the Roman remains had been found rather than at the museum. If he was wrong, he would have another journey to make. He ran for as long as he could, then slowed to a brisk walk when he needed a rest. But it took him a while even so. He wondered what the others were doing – counting Roman coins, or trying again to communicate with the soldiers, or . . .

As he neared his destination, his mind turned to what he would say to Mr Worthington when he found him. More and more, he began to wonder if he should have gone to the Myton Museum instead. It was possible that Mr Worthington would be sorting and examining the finds from the excavation.

Eventually he trudged up the shallow incline to the woods in Hawthorne Crescent Gardens. The clouds had thinned, so at least he could see where he was going. He was careful not to trip in the long grass. Was that a light in among the trees? Or was it merely the moon reflecting off something? Surely there would be a policeman around to guard the site, at the very least.

There was. The burly figure stepped out from the trees and grabbed the startled Jonny by the arm.

'Now then, young man, where do you think you're going?'

Jonny tried to shake off the policeman's hold, but without success. 'I'm looking for Mr Worthington. I have a message for him.'

'Mr Worthington, eh?'

'From the museum.'

'I know who Mr Worthington is,' the policeman snapped back.

Jonny pulled away, afraid the man was going to cuff his ear. But instead the policeman let him go.

'You were here yesterday,' the policeman said. 'With Lord Fotherington.'

'That's right. We came with Mr Worthington and Charlie.'

'He might be Charlie to you, but he's Lord Fotherington to us mere mortals.' There was the slightest hint of respect now in the policeman's voice. He waved a hand in the direction of the trees. 'Worthington's in there somewhere, poking about with his trowel.'

'Thank you.' Jonny set off quickly into the trees.

'Mind how you go,' the policeman called after him. 'They've dug holes and all sorts.'

Picking his way through the gloom of the wood, Jonny almost fell into a trench that had been dug right across a clearing. It was just a black strip in the ground and his foot caught the edge of it. He only just managed to pull back before he slipped in. He had no idea how deep it was and he didn't want to find out.

'Careful – you'll ruin everything blundering about like that.'

Jonny recognised Mr Worthington's voice at once. 'It's me, Jonny Levin,' he called back. 'Er, how's it going?' he added, unsure what he was going to say to persuade the man to come with him to Northerton.

Worthington's face emerged smiling from the gloom. 'Wish I'd brought a torch. It's got so dark. Raincoat wouldn't have gone amiss either, come to that,' he said. 'Everyone else has gone and left me to it now, I'm afraid. Just packing up myself.'

'Have you found much?' Jonny asked.

'Well, yes, you could say that.' He sounded unsure. 'It's all a bit curious, though. Lots of stuff close to the surface, but none of the lower evidence and detritus you would expect from such an important find.'

'As if the relics were just dumped here?' Jonny suggested.

'Obviously they were dumped – the people

burying them were probably in a hurry to get away from Boudicca's rebels – but . . .'

'I meant recently,' Jonny said.

Worthington laughed. 'That would explain a lot,' he said. 'But it's not terribly likely, now, is it?'

'What if . . .' Jonny said slowly. 'What if I could show you where all this stuff was brought from – the coins and bones and everything.'

'Brought *from*? You mean recently? You really do?'

Jonny nodded solemnly. 'I do. We've found the rest of the treasure.'

Worthington's eyes were gleaming with excitement. 'The *rest* of it? Oh, my word, that is a turn-up. I always said that Stepney was an unlikely location for such a rich find.' He was nodding. 'Though why anyone would move things round . . . Take things for themselves, yes, I understand that, though obviously I can't condone it. But just moving it? For what purpose?'

'Art has an idea about that.' Jonny led the way back out of the woods, watching his feet carefully. 'And there's lots of other things we need to show you too.' He paused, as a thought

179

occurred to him. 'Can you speak Latin? Because if not, we need to find someone who can.'

'Speak it? Not much call for that. I read it, of course. Don't tell me you've found documents? Inscriptions? Oh, this is marvellous.' He clapped his hands together and shuffled his feet in an approximation of a jig – to the amusement of the policeman, who was watching from close by.

'Something like that,' Jonny said. 'You'll see. It's quite a walk, I'm afraid.'

'Walk?' Worthington sounded scandalised. 'We'll get a taxi, thank you.'

The soldiers stood to attention in the shadows. Their leader had made no further effort to communicate with Art and the others. It was amazing how the figures seemed to fade into the night, Art thought. Unless you looked right at them as they stood in the shadows, you wouldn't know they were there.

So it did not surprise him that, when Jonny and Worthington finally arrived, the little man did not notice the soldiers at all – despite walking right past two of them.

Flinch and Meg were inside the mausoleum,

talking quietly. Art met Jonny midway along the path through the graveyard.

'I think we'll show Mr Worthington the mausoleum before anything else,' he said to Jonny.

They watched with a mixture of interest and amusement as Worthington stared at the pile of artefacts. Art almost laughed as the little man stooped down to examine the coins. He was shaking his head in disbelief.

'And someone just dug it up, with no thought for preserving the integrity of the site,' he said sadly. 'Dumped it in here. I wonder why.'

'We think they were worried it might attract attention,' Meg said.

'It certainly would. Someone who wants to let the dead rest in peace, is that it? RIP, *Requiescat in pace.*' He straightened up. 'Speaking of which, Jonny here said there were some documents, in Latin.'

Jonny coughed. 'Er, that isn't quite what I said.'

Worthington's face fell. 'No documents?'

'We do need a translator,' Art told him. 'But it's a little more complicated than just Latin writing.'

'You intrigue me. What can it be?'

'You'll never guess,' Flinch said, grinning. 'You won't.'

Art led the way back outside. As they approached the leading soldier, Worthington gave a gasp.

'My word, what a terrific costume. You know, it looks exactly right.' He stopped and turned to Art. 'Now, you've not been messing about, have you?' he demanded severely. 'You could damage the armour if you don't know how to put it on. Funny, though,' he continued, turning back to face the soldier, 'I would expect it to look older. This armour is polished like new.'

The soldier stared back at Worthington. '*Vide et credere*,' he said. His words seemed to echo round the graveyard.

'Oh, excellent!' Worthington was delighted. 'Yes, very good indeed.'

'But what does it mean?' Flinch asked.

'What? Oh, come on, I'm sure you can ask the gentleman yourself,' Worthington said. 'Very amusing.'

'She's serious,' Art said. 'We don't under-stand him.' He gestured to the other soldiers. 'Or any of them.'

Worthington could see now that there were others. 'You have gone to a lot of trouble,' he said. 'And, as I'm sure you know full well, "*vide et credere*" means "see and believe". You know,' he went on, oblivious to the children's sighs and exchanged looks, 'this armour really is most magnificent. May I?' He reached out to touch the breastplate.

And his hand went through it.

With a start of surprise, Worthington pulled his hand away. Then slowly, gently, he prodded again – this time at the soldier's arm. Again, his hand went through.

The soldier laughed. '*Nihili est*,' he barked. Then he slapped his own hand across Worthington's face – across it and through it.

'Oh, my giddy aunt,' Worthington said in a faint voice. 'What is going on here?'

'We were hoping you would ask him that,' Art said. 'Since you're the only one who can understand what the ghost of a Roman soldier says.'

Worthington's face was shining in the pale light as he translated the soldier's words.

I, Gaius Julius Atreus, centurion of the personal guard to the Governor, Suetonius Paulinus, was given charge of the special cohort.

This was in the year when the Queen of the Britons, Boudicca, rebelled against the rule of Rome. She had to be stopped as she sacked town after town, putting the innocent to the sword and proclaiming the end of the Empire.

But she had more than mere enthusiasm and brutality on her side. We knew, from our spies and from the boasts of prisoners taken in the battles, that Boudicca's Witchmen had cast a powerful spell for her.

The gods of the Britons were as nothing compared with our own gods, of course. But the spell was powerful. The Witchmen conjured a force – a being of pure energy – by their appeals to the ancient pagan gods. They appealed to this force to help them in their fight – to be their strength and sword, to smite the Roman Empire and reclaim the lands of Britain for the original inhabitants.

They called this creature 'Darkening', for thus it was. A cloud of black hatred that hung heavy in the air above the battle and killed our legionaries with its very touch. And so Paulinus and his advisers decided on a plan. As Boudicca and her Iceni warriors marched on Londinium, leaving Verulamium and other cities in smoke and flames, so I was charged with destroying the Darkening.

I chose a dozen men, all soldiers who had served under me with great skill and bravery. Together we were the Special Force — the Numeri — so called, as only we had the power to hold back the Darkening. We knew from a Witchman who did not follow Boudicca that the Darkening drains the life of men. It feeds on their souls and bodies and takes the very energy that binds us together. But a dedicated group of great spirit and determination could hold this force in check.

We could tame the Darkening and keep it in thrall — by sacrificing our own energies. Our own lives. We prepared to use the elements of the world itself — earth, air, fire and water.

And so, even as Boudicca reached Londinium, we engaged the Darkening in this place. Though it has changed much, I see it is still a place of death. We bound the Darkening using the rituals and chants the Witchman taught us. We held our ground, despite the taunts of Boudicca's wise men and the power that sapped our souls. We stood firm on the earth the witchman had prepared beneath our feet and enclosed the Darkening in a stone casket that the Witchman had blessed for us, binding it tight with spells and sealing it for ever inside. Trapped with a little air, sealed with the heat of fire. With my sword – this sword, wrought from mountain iron by the fire of the Witchman of Paulinus himself – I smote the Darkening and weakened it. Then we buried it in the earth, close to the great river, since we knew that the power of water would dilute and weaken the Darkening. We buried it deep, so it might be entombed for ever.

Or so we thought.

But now we have been recalled to this place, so the Darkening cannot be far away.

And that is our enduring task. Each of the thirteen of us was handsomely paid for our services. The treasure was buried with us, for after we had entombed the Darkening only our bones remained – bleached clean by its

186

destructive power. They — we — were buried here, with our payment. And also the casket, so that we might watch over it for all eternity.

But now I sense that the casket has been breached. Soon it will be opened and, unless we intervene, the Darkening will emerge once more to destroy the impure, the colonists, the immigrants, those foreign to the ancient gods of the Iceni tribe. Yet we are depleted. Some of my Numeri are missing, gone from this place. And without them, we cannot overcome. Without our full strength we can never defeat the Darkening, and chaos will rule triumphant.

Deep underground, in the tunnels beneath the murky waters of the River Thames, a hand caressed the rough, aged stone of the casket.

A hand wearing a ring depicting two inter-twined snakes. Augustus Bablock felt carefully along the tiny crack in the stone. His fingers searched for a catch or a clasp. He examined every inch of the casket through darkening blood-shot eyes.

To Arthur's amazement, his grandad had been following the underwater adventures of Martin Michael with interest.

'We're both stuck in little boxes,' Grandad joked, looking round his small room in the home. 'Difference is, he's got a view.'

Grandad's room looked out on to the red-brick wall of the next building.

'Look, they're starting,' Sarah said excitedly.

She turned up the volume of the small television that perched on a table in the corner of the room. The picture showed the crane operator inside his cabin. In an effort to seem clever, the camera moved outside the crane, up and along its arm, then down the chain and cables into the water.

The Thames was bubbling at the point where the chain went in. As they watched, the glassy lid of Michael's box appeared. It was tilted slightly and, as the rest of the box emerged, muddy water running off and splashing back into the river below, Michael himself could be seen hunched up in a corner of his glass cube. A close-up revealed that he had his hands over his eyes.

'Probably not used to the light,' Sarah said.

'He's usually posing in shades,' Arthur pointed out. 'Thinks it makes him look cool or trendy or something.'

Sarah did not reply. She picked up a newspaper she had brought with her. The cover declared that inside was exclusive information about Michael's 'Incredible Week of Bravery'. She opened it quickly to the spread about the stunt.

'It says in here that they're going to give him dark glasses for a time when he comes out.'

'I haven't seen that,' Grandad said. 'May I?'

She handed him the paper, folded open to the right page. Arthur shook his head and sighed. Sarah was again glued to the screen and Grandad was now reading the paper with obvious interest.

As Grandad held it up, angling the page so it got the best light, Arthur could see the other half of the article on the back, where the paper was folded. There was a large photo of the clump of weed or shadow or whatever it was – a still taken from the camera footage. Next to it was another, very similar but rather clearer picture. He struggled to read the caption as Grandad shifted and the paper moved.

'Hold still a mo.'

'What is it?' Grandad asked, lowering the paper so that Arthur couldn't read it at all.

'Oh, nothing. A computer-enhanced picture of that whatever it was. Says it could actually be a hand, but they still can't tell.'

Grandad turned the paper over, and Sarah managed to leave the telly for long enough to join them and take a look.

'It is a lot like a hand,' she admitted. 'See, the fingers.' She traced her own finger along the enhanced photograph. She paused, halfway down what might have been the fourth finger. 'I don't know what that is, though.'

Arthur peered closely at the picture. 'Just a shadow. Or something the computer's tried to make out of one.' He turned his head from side to side, in case changing the angle helped. 'Could be a ring, I suppose,' he admitted.

'It is.' Grandad's voice was quiet, but it had a serious edge to it now that Arthur had not heard for a while.

'It can't be,' Sarah said, turning back to the screen.

'It is a ring,' Grandad insisted. He tapped his own, gnarled and weathered finger on the picture. 'A large ring, with a round, flat emblem embossed on it.' He traced gently over what Arthur had taken to be ripples in the water. 'See?'

'It looks like a snake,' Arthur realised. 'Or rather, two snakes, intertwined.'

Grandad nodded. 'Yes,' he said. 'That's exactly what it is.'

CHAPTER NINE

The night hung like a cloud over the graveyard. The moon was gone and all that remained were the shadows – the vague silhouettes of the Roman soldiers, the children sitting on the stone surround of a grave, the historian frozen midway between disbelief and excitement. And the centurion, the horsehair plumes of his helmet bristling in the breeze as he solidified out of the shadows.

Worthington reached out and tapped the centurion on the breastplate. 'I can touch you now,' he said, quickly translating this into Latin for the centurion's benefit. 'I noticed that he was getting wet from the rain even when I couldn't touch him before,' he said to Art and the others. 'Perhaps there are degrees of transparency, or insubstantiation.' He shook his head and sighed. 'This is a lot to take in.'

'But it doesn't matter, does it?' Meg said. 'Even if it's true, all this stuff about the Darkening killing anyone who's an invader. I mean, we all live here. No one's invading now, are they?'

'Could be jolly useful,' Jonny said, 'if Herr Hitler looks this way.'

Art was watching Worthington's troubled expression. 'You don't seem so sure.'

'No no no,' the historian said. He tapped his chin with his index finger. 'I don't think it's good at all. Assuming it isn't all a fairy story, of course.' He glanced at the centurion, huge and impassive behind him. 'Not that I think it is,' he added hastily, even though the Romans could not understand him. 'No, the problem is that the Iceni tribe is long gone. So far as this Darkening is able to tell, we're *all* invaders now. Every one of us is impure in the sense that our bloodlines, our ancestry, have mingled with the Romans, the Vikings, the Norman French, immigrants and invaders from almost every part of the world.'

Flinch jumped to her feet. 'You mean it will kill everyone?'

Worthington nodded. 'I think it may come to that, yes,' he said sadly.

He glanced back at the Roman soldiers, and Jonny could see how nervous the man was.

'Then we've got to stop it,' Flinch announced.

'And we do have help,' Art pointed out. He gestured to the centurion. 'They stopped this thing before, they can stop it again. Before it ever gets out, if we're lucky and we act now.'

Worthington nodded, and spoke rapidly to the centurion. The Roman shook his head and replied. Art and the others waited eagerly for the translation.

'I'm afraid there is a problem,' Worthington announced. 'There should be thirteen soldiers in all, thirteen Numeri, as Gaius Atreus here refers to them.' He pointed to the shadowy outlines of the other Romans. 'There are only eight. They have, somehow, lost five of their men. He also urges us to hurry up with whatever we are doing, as there may be very little time before this Darkening thing escapes.'

'Of course,' Jonny said suddenly. He leaped to his feet. 'The soldiers were buried with the casket to sort of guard it, weren't they?'

'So it would seem.'

'And as the Darkening is recalled or wakes up or whatever, so the soldiers are woken too, to balance things.'

'Yes, but the balance has been thrown off,' Art said. He turned to Worthington. 'Isn't that right? So now the Darkening can escape.'

'But don't you see?' Jonny said excitedly. 'The bodies aren't buried with the casket any longer. At least, not all of them.'

Art did see. He realised what Jonny was saying. 'Bablock moved the bodies. Along with some of the treasure, he dug up some of the bodies and moved them too.'

'That bone we found,' Meg said as she too realised.

'Who is Bablock?' Worthington asked.

'He's the forger,' Flinch said. 'He's got printing presses and coin-making machines in his tunnel under the river. You get to it through a tomb.'

Worthington just stared at her. 'I did think that this was as complicated as it could get,' he said quietly. 'Perhaps you can tell me later. In the meantime, Jonny's right. We've found the bodies, or partial bodies, of five men. And, as Jonny so eloquently put it to me earlier this evening, they looked as though they'd just been dumped in the woods in Stepney.'

'Then perhaps we need to bring them back here and give them a proper burial with their fellows,' Art said.

With a nod, Worthington turned and spoke to the centurion. From the tone of the conversation, even though he didn't understand a word of it, Art could tell that he was right. The bodies had to be brought back.

They decided on a division of labour. Mr Worthington was the obvious one to supervise the return of the bodies to the graveyard. Art was keen to know what was happening in the tunnel – what Bablock was up to. Both he and Jonny had seen the man's eyes turn black, but how much had he been infected by the Darkening the centurion had described? Was he poisoned, or possessed? Since Art and Flinch had been down in the tunnel before, it was sensible for them to be the ones to go back and see what was happening and to find the stone casket.

'Are you sure, Flinch?' Art asked. 'You don't have to come, you know. I can go on my own, or one of the others . . .'

But Flinch was insistent. 'I'll come,' she said, and from her tone of voice and her expression Art knew there was no point trying to dissuade her.

Which left Meg and Jonny to help

Worthington transport the bodies back from Stepney. They all went to the tomb and watched Art and Flinch start down the steps. Now that Art knew how to open it up again, they did not have to worry about being there to help them out on their return.

'How will we get the bodies back?' Jonny wondered as they set off for Stepney, keeping a lookout for a cab.

'We can hardly put them in a taxi,' Worthington thought.

'Unless we crate them up or something,' Meg said.

'Bablock's men used a wheelbarrow, at least for some of the way,' Jonny remembered.

'Get Art's dad to organise a police car maybe?' Meg suggested.

'Art's dad?' Worthington said.

'He's a policeman, a detective,' Jonny explained. 'But I doubt he'd be very impressed with our story. It would take too long to convince him.'

'I'm inclined to agree,' Worthington said. 'I think we head for the museum and pick up some heavy bags. It may not be terribly respectful to bundle the poor soldiers' bones all up together, but it does seem the most expeditious solution.'

The policeman at the woods in Stepney helped them put the bones into bags. He didn't seem at all surprised that two children were helping Worthington with archaeological research in the early evening.

The bodies – just bones now – had been laid out on the ground where they were uncovered. Close by, the remnants of the soldiers' armour was carefully arranged, ready to be catalogued.

'Do we need this?' Jonny wondered, pointing to the armour.

'Possibly not,' Worthington said. 'If things don't, er, work out,' he went on, watching the policeman's reaction as he spoke, 'then we can always come back for it later.'

The policeman nodded as if he quite understood. 'I'll be here all night, sir. Till Rawlings takes over at eight o'clock.'

'You're very kind,' Worthington told him. 'Now, if you will forgive us, we must be getting on.'

They made a final sweep of the excavation with the policeman's torch, but there seemed to be no more bones.

'Let's hope that's all of them,' Jonny said.

Together they carried the heavy bags down to the road. Worthington had told the taxi to wait and the driver was sitting there. He started the engine as they appeared.

'Back to Northerton,' Worthington said as they struggled into the back of the cab with their bags.

'Right you are, guv.'

The cab started into the night.

A short while later Worthington paid off the curious cab driver, who seemed ready to keep the engine idling while he parked outside the graveyard to watch what was going on. Jonny, Meg and Worthington waited outside the gate for fully a minute, then made a pretence of walking slowly up the road, their hessian sacks over their shoulders as if they were coalmen. The driver eventually got bored and soon headlights bit through the mist that had replaced the earlier rain as he drove away.

'I thought he'd never go,' Meg said.

'Are you all right to help?' Jonny asked. 'Only I know you like to get home before it's too late.'

Meg bit her lower lip as she considered. 'It'll be all right,' she decided, honouring Jonny with the faintest of smiles. 'The pubs don't close for a while yet. And,' she went on determinedly, 'this is important.'

Once back in the graveyard, Worthington hurried to speak to the centurion. He was standing, watching, exactly as and where they had left him.

'He doesn't seem to think it matters where we put the bones, so long as they are here, in the graveyard – the place of death, as he calls it.'

So they emptied the bags out on the muddy ground beside the mausoleum. The soldiers stepped out of the shadows, coming closer to watch – forming a circle round Jonny and the others as they emptied out the dry, brittle bones. They seemed to glow in the pale light of the moon diffused through the clouds.

There was a sound, like the wind in the trees, except that the night was still – the mist was not moving and the trees stood impassive and immobile. Jonny looked round. The centurion, he saw, was smiling and nodding.

In the gaps in the circle of soldiers, more figures were slowly materialising, as if being formed from the mist itself. The grey became black, filled out, grew features and detail. Another Roman legionary stood to attention beside his fellows. And another. Then a third . . .

Worthington was shaking with delight, hands clenched into fists in front of his face. He counted round the circle – nodding at each of the Romans in turn: '*Unus, duo, tres, quattuor, quinque, sex, septem, octo, novem, decem, undecim, duodecim* . . .' He stopped, his finger pointing to an empty space.

Jonny strained to see through the mist. Was there a figure there? The ghost of a figure maybe – hazy and insubstantial.

'What has happened to *tredecim*?' Worthington wondered quietly.

'We're missing some bones,' Meg said.

'Perhaps only one bone,' Worthington agreed. 'That might be enough to . . .'

He turned to the centurion, but the soldier

was already shaking his head sadly even before Worthington spoke to him.

'They really do need all thirteen working together,' Worthington confirmed. 'Twelve doesn't give them the power they need apparently. More's the pity.'

'So what do we do?' Meg asked. 'Spend for ever looking for the last bones?'

Worthington sighed. 'I really don't think there can be any more bones at Stepney. Given that they were merely placed there, we will have found them all, I'm sure.' He sighed. 'I would ask your friend Art. He seems to have the best idea of what's going on.' He frowned and checked his watch. 'I'm surprised he and Flinch aren't back yet. They've been gone a very long time.'

'Perhaps they're in trouble,' Meg said. 'Do you think we should go and see?'

'Far too dangerous,' Worthington replied. While looking for the cab that took them to Stepney, they had recounted Art and Flinch's tale of what they had found in the tunnels. 'Especially if this man Bablock has now been infected or something by this Darkening business.'

'We can't just kick our heels and do nothing,' Jonny said.

He was getting frustrated and worried. Worthington was right – Art and Flinch must have been gone for ages. He and Meg and Worthington had been to Stepney and back since they went down into the tunnel again. What could be happening?

'I agree with Jonny,' Meg said. 'We have to tell Art's dad or Charlie or someone. Whether they believe us or not, and no matter how long it takes.'

'I'll go,' Jonny said. 'Charlie may be at home, and it's not far off the way to Scotland Yard.'

'Perhaps we should look for a cab,' Worthington said.

'Jonny'll be quicker,' Meg promised, and Jonny grinned.

'Oh, very well,' Worthington conceded. 'Then I shall take a quick look down that tomb of yours and see what is happening in the tunnel.'

'Just you and Meg?' Jonny said, surprised. He could see that Meg was looking slightly pale at the thought.

'Good gracious me, no. Someone has to stay

here in case Art and Flinch return, and to be here when you get back, Jonny. I shall go alone.'

They both tried to talk him out of it, but Worthington was determined. He insisted he would take a quick look and be back as soon as he could to await Jonny and reinforcements. 'Better to know the lie of the land, though, eh?' he said, rubbing his hands together. 'From what Art was saying, it sounds like an old tram tunnel. A Royal Commission proposed a subterranean tramway system about thirty years ago. That's when they built the Kingsway tram tunnel. But after that the idea sort of petered out. Sounds fascinating.' He turned to Jonny. 'Now then, I doubt if even you are quick enough to be able to afford to hang about here nattering.'

Jonny took the point. He allowed Meg to give him a quick hug by way of a farewell, then he set off through the mist towards Charlie's house. He enjoyed running, and the loneliness and still of the night made it all the more exhilarating. The mist parted for him as his feet echoed off the damp pavements and cobbles and the cool night air rushed past his ears.

As he ran, Jonny thought back over the

events of the last few days. He thought about the ghostly Roman soldiers and their gruff centurion – was a great darkness really about to be unleashed on London? He thought about the mausoleum and the treasure all but abandoned there. He thought about Worthington's enthusiasm for finding the smallest relic of the past compared with the bored men who had wheelbarrowed the artefacts from the graveyard. They had not even bothered to stop when they dropped something, they were that slapdash about it all.

He paused for breath when he reached the front door. The journey had seemed to take only a few minutes, though he was sure it must have been longer. There was a light on inside the house, which was a good sign. And for all the frenetic activity of the afternoon and evening, it was still early after all. He pressed the bell and heard it ring somewhere deep inside the house.

Then he waited. It seemed to be taking an age for anyone to come. After the speed of his journey from Northerton, Jonny was soon convinced that he had waited hours. He rang the bell again.

And as his finger pressed the button, he realised how stupid he had been. He had remembered – recalled in his mind's eye – the bone they had found lying in the street, the bone that Art had taken and examined, which had seemed such a clue.

The bone that was now back at the Cannoniers' den.

The bone that might just be the final part of the spell that would bring the Roman soldiers back from the dead to defeat the Darkening.

Jonny stared at the impassive front door of the house. He strained to hear if anyone was coming. Should he wait? Or should he get back to the den and retrieve that last bone just as fast as he could?

'Be serious,' Sarah insisted. 'It's just a smudge. The whole thing is smudged.'

Grandad and Arthur were still examining the picture.

'I don't think it's smudged,' Grandad said.

'The computer would have unsmudged it, surely? You know about computers,' Arthur said to Sarah. 'Wouldn't it have taken any smudging away?'

'Oh, for goodness' sake.' She didn't turn from the screen, which showed Martin Michael giving a news conference on the Embankment beside his glass box. To Arthur's amusement and amazement, she was recording it on the video built into Grandad's little telly. 'It's underwater,' Sarah was saying. 'It's a bit of weed or a shadow or something.'

'Wearing a ring,' Arthur pointed out.

'Emanating darkness,' Grandad added.

Michael sounded surprisingly healthy after his ordeal. He was explaining about how much he had enjoyed – or not – being fed puréed fruit and vegetables down a tube for a week.

'Darkness?' Arthur was getting worried now. 'You don't think . . .'

'No, he doesn't,' Sarah said loudly. 'And neither do you. I mean, after all this time and everything, it's just daft to assume . . .' Her voice tailed off.

'Assume what?' Arthur asked.

'Did you see that?' Sarah said, pointing to the telly.

'What?' Arthur asked.

Grandad shrugged. Michael seemed to be

cutting the session short, saying he was tired and leaving. He had another appointment, he revealed, to the evident amusement of several of the journalists.

Sarah hesitated, then hit the stop button on the video.

'You'll lose your precious recording,' Arthur pointed out, but Sarah waved at him to be quiet.

She pressed Play, then rewound back through the last few seconds of the news conference.

'Here, now. Look,' Sarah said. She sounded slightly breathless.

As he answered, Michael waved a hand in the air. 'It's just, you know, *mush*.' His hand caught the side of his sunglasses, knocking them slightly. They tilted, falling down his nose and exposing his eyes, just for a moment. The picture froze as he pushed them back up.

'You see?'

'See what?' Arthur said.

But Grandad was nodding grimly. 'Show it again,' he said.

Sarah replayed the sequence once more. But this time she managed to freeze the image as Michael's glasses slipped away.

Michael remained frozen on the screen, looking out at Arthur, Sarah and Grandad. Staring at them through eyes as black as night.

CHAPTER TEN

There was no sign of Bablock as Art and Flinch crept along the tunnel. Art risked using his torch for the darkened section, switching it off when they reached the area that was lit. But they moved slowly and cautiously, pausing between every footstep to listen and check that no one was coming. After an age, they reached the point where the main tunnel split. As before, they followed the service tunnel to the side, keeping out of the sight of the men working at the counterfeiting machines.

'Where's he taken the casket?' Flinch asked.

Art shook his head. 'No idea. Maybe there are rooms or something off the tunnel further up. Or maybe we'll see him if we keep going.'

In fact, they heard Bablock before they saw him. He was talking again to the quieter man, Galman, in the main tunnel. Bablock was shouting to be heard above the noise of the machine beside them – above the sound of the whirring engine and the 'chink' of forged coins as they clattered into the collecting tray.

'I've been thinking about that padlock,'

Bablock was saying. 'We cannot afford to be found. Especially not now.'

Flinch and Art crept closer, standing on the other side of the pillar from the men, straining to hear. Art risked a quick look round the pillar. Bablock was framed against the backdrop of busy machines and working men. Art could see that the man's irises were charcoal black.

Galman too seemed to have noticed the eyes. He was unable to look away from Bablock's face. 'Yes, sir.' He sounded nervous.

'I want men posted at the end of the tunnel. Just in case anyone finds the way in.'

'Oh, surely that isn't likely,' Galman replied. Still he was staring at Bablock's face. But he took a step backwards as Bablock's features twisted into a snarl.

'Just do it!' Bablock shouted furiously. 'Don't you dare question me, Galman – you hear? Just do it!'

Galman swallowed. His voice was stretched out taut, shaking. 'Of course, sir.' He did not move.

'What are you waiting for?' Bablock demanded. 'What are you staring at?'

'Nothing, sir. Nothing,' Galman said quickly, looking down at his feet.

'My eyes, perhaps?' Bablock's voice was quiet now, and to Art it sounded all the more dangerous for it. 'You are wondering about my eyes.'

Galman laughed, but it was a forced, joyless sound. 'Of course not.'

'Of course not,' Bablock echoed. 'Perhaps I have spent too long underground. The darkness has reached even my eyes.'

'I – I'll send someone to guard the entrance,' Galman said. He nodded quickly, turned and walked away.

Flinch was tugging at Art's sleeve. 'If they guard the way in,' she whispered, 'then that means we can't get out. We're trapped down here.'

Art nodded, but he was still watching Bablock. As the man turned to go, Art saw that under his arm he was carrying the stone casket from the mausoleum.

'Come on, Flinch,' Art said quietly. 'Let's see where he goes.'

They hurried quietly along the service tunnel, pausing at each pillar before running quickly and quietly across the arched gap to the next, hoping no one would see them. Each time they were in the open, Art expected to hear shouts, for people to point. He glanced into the main tunnel, keeping track of Bablock's progress. Sometimes he was hurrying onwards, sometimes he had paused to talk to one of the men or to check a machine, examining the coins and notes dropping into the collecting trays.

'Where's he off to?' Flinch wondered.

'To the other end of the tunnel perhaps,' Art thought. 'Maybe there's a way out at the other side of the river.'

The sound of laughter alerted them to the danger ahead. Art and Flinch both froze as they heard it. Then two men stepped into the service tunnel.

'Quick!'

Art pulled Flinch into cover beside the pillar they had been hiding behind. Luckily there was a machine close inside the main tunnel, and they were able to duck down there. No one seemed to be looking their way.

'We'll lose him,' Flinch whispered.

'I hope not.'

Art risked a quick look over the top of the

machine. It seemed that Flinch might be right. Bablock was walking quickly down the tunnel now. Soon he would disappear into the gloom as the lighting again diminished once he left the main working area.

'They're coming this way,' Flinch whispered close to Art's ear as he ducked down again. He could barely hear her above the metallic punching of the machine. 'They'll see us!'

Art peered round the pillar, aware of Flinch's head just below his own as she did the same. The sound of the machine diminished and he could at once hear the men laughing and talking. They were very close, and both Art and Flinch whipped their heads quickly back. Another few steps and the men would surely see them both, even if they stayed absolutely still and silent.

He took another look round the machine, into the main tunnel. There were men working everywhere – dozens of them. But they did all seem to be occupied, busy at machines, examining notes and coins, and writing on clipboards.

Art grabbed Flinch's hand and pulled her, still crouched, out. He just hoped he had timed it right. Together they ran quickly round the machine and the pillar, and flattened themselves against the opposite wall – just as the two men passed, their backs now to Art and Flinch.

For the moment, he thought, they were safe. He was pretty sure they had made it unseen.

'Sorry, Flinch,' he said, 'but I think we lost Bablock.'

'We'll find him,' she said.

'Well, we know which way he was heading.'

Art was about to lead her on down the service tunnel when the shouting started. Immediately the two of them flattened themselves behind the pillar.

'They saw us,' Flinch said, her eyes wide. She was looking round, searching for a way of escape. 'Shall we run for it?'

Art hesitated. They might run straight into the people shouting for them. And they now knew the way out of the tunnel was guarded. But if they had been seen, where could they possibly hide?

The shouting was coming closer. Art frowned and held tight to Flinch's hand. Strangely, though, while the sound was coming along the tunnel, it did not seem to be heading directly for them. He had expected people to appear either side of the pillar, to start running along the service tunnel, to yell at them to stop . . . But it sounded more like swearing and struggling.

Art could hear one voice raised above the others: 'Let me go. How dare you? Take your hands off me this instant. I shall make a formal complaint about this, I can tell you . . .' It was a voice that Art recognised.

Flinch was looking out into the main tunnel again. She turned back to Art, her face pale and her tone urgent. 'They've got Mr Worthington,' she said.

As the struggling group drew level with the pillar, Art could see she was right. Mr Worthington was being dragged along the tunnel by several of Bablock's men. He was trying to shake off their grip and pull himself free, but they held him tight.

'Quit your shouting,' one of the men bellowed, and Art recognised the gruff voice of the man who had been with Bablock and Galman in the mausoleum. 'You can complain all you like to Mr Bablock.'

'They're taking him to Bablock,' Flinch hissed. 'Can't we help him?'

'Not yet. There are too many people. We'll see.'

Art watched the group disappearing down the tunnel, following where Bablock had gone earlier.

Everyone seemed to be looking at the men dragging Worthington with them, so it was much easier for Art and Flinch to follow along the service tunnel without fear of being spotted. At the end of the working area where the machines were set up, the lighting diminished – the bulbs were strung further apart, the glow from one barely meeting the light from the next. The service tunnel ended abruptly in a brick wall, and Flinch and Art were forced to rejoin the main concourse. The lack of illumination helped them as they flitted from shadow to shadow. Worthington's continuing protests floated back to them from the gloom ahead.

A patch of light appeared in the tunnel before them. A bright yellow rectangle that seemed to open in the air. A door, Art realised – giving into a well-lit room. He and Flinch stood motionless in a patch of shadow and watched as the men dragged Worthington inside. The door was pushed shut behind them.

But it did not completely close. Art and Flinch ran to the side of the door and Art put his finger to his lips. He did not dare to look into the room, but they could hear clearly enough what was going on inside.

'I demand that you release me at once,' Worthington was saying loudly. 'How dare you, sir? I'll have you know that—'

But Bablock cut him off, his voice echoing with anger. 'And I'll have you know that you were trespassing. I am quite within my rights to hold you here indefinitely.'

Worthington gave a dismissive snort. 'I very much doubt that. And counterfeiting is a criminal offence, so the accusation of trespass doesn't really hold water, now, does it?'

'If I am a criminal, then you should guard your tongue,' Bablock snapped back. 'Marsden – was he alone?'

'Seemed to be,' the man with the gruff voice replied.

'You'd better check. If there are others, then we must deal with them too. Or else we shall have to . . .' His voice tailed off.

'Sir?'

'Never mind. I doubt it will come to that. Just take these men with you and check, Marsden.' This was followed by a chuckle. 'It's all right, I have my gun. This gentleman will be quite safe with me.'

Art and Flinch drew back into the deepest shadows as the door started to open again.

'And send Galman here,' Bablock shouted after the men who were emerging from the room. 'With a hammer.'

As soon as the men had gone, Art and Flinch returned to the door. It was still standing slightly open and Art peered carefully inside. He was surprised to see that the room beyond looked like an ordinary office. There was a large wooden desk, several filing cabinets, even a painting on the wall – a painting of Bablock. Beside the painting, mounted on the wall, were two metal boxes. Each had a large lever attached to the side and Art guessed they controlled the lighting. A main switch, perhaps, to plunge the tunnels into darkness.

Bablock was sitting at the desk. His hands were resting on the large blotter, one of them holding a revolver that was pointed at Worthington.

There was a lamp on the desk, angled into Worthington's face as he stood on the other side. Art was not sure if this was to dazzle Worthington or to throw Bablock's features into shadow. Even so, he could see the black circles that were now the man's pupils. They seemed larger than they had before.

On the desk beside the blotter was the stone casket. Running across the top and down one side, Art could see the black line of a crack.

'I was quite alone, you know,' Worthington said quietly.

'Really? We shall see.' Bablock's free hand moved across to the casket and gently stroked along the line of the crack. 'I can't afford to be found now, you know. I must survive – we must survive.'

'We?' Worthington nodded. He seemed to have regained his usual composure. 'Ah, you mean yourself and your new friend. The Darkening.'

The revolver jabbed forwards and Bablock's face twisted into an angry stare. 'What do you know about that?' His voice was a hoarse whisper.

'Everything,' Worthington whispered back.

The dark eyes narrowed. 'I doubt that . . . And I am not sure you really are alone.'

'I assure you that I am.'

'And if you are not,' Bablock went on, 'then I may have to take drastic measures.'

'Oh?'

Bablock rose slowly to his feet, keeping the gun levelled at Worthington. He went over to the portrait, sparing it a glance. 'If you did have anyone with you, they will never get in. I can have the flood gates closed at either end of the tunnel. It would take days for anyone to get through them.'

'Are you sure?'

He reached up to the two large switches. 'Oh, yes, I'm sure. But even if I weren't, this switch –' he reached up and tapped one on the right – 'this controls the explosive charges that are positioned at intervals along the tunnel. I can set a timer, or blow them instantly. Of course, I would leave myself long enough to get out of this end of the tunnel before the Thames made short work of whoever had managed to get in at the other. And anyone else left behind down here . . .'

*

The mist was becoming a cold fog. Meg stamped her feet and hugged her arms round herself, hoping that Jonny, or Art and Flinch, or Mr Worthington – or anyone – would be back soon.

The Roman soldiers stood in their circle, one space still remaining. Their eyes seemed to follow Meg wherever she went, though she thought this might just be her imagination. The way that the eyes in portraits seemed to follow you round the room.

She had tried talking to the centurion, but he had smiled grimly and shaken his head, obviously unable to understand anything she said. When he had spoken, it meant nothing to her either, so they simply shrugged at each other and gave up.

Just as she had got to the point of wondering if she should also descend into the tunnel and try to find out what was going on, the cars arrived. She heard them first – the jangle of bells. Then the headlights cutting through the fog. The dark shapes screeched up outside the gate and equally dark figures emerged, hurrying into the grave-yard.

'Meg!' Art's dad – Detective Sergeant Drake – was the first of the men. 'Lord Fotherington called me, with a message from Jonny about counterfeiters.' He looked round the graveyard, taking a step backwards as he saw the circle of Romans. 'He didn't say they were in fancy dress, though.'

'Those aren't the forgers,' Meg said. 'They're . . .' She hesitated. 'They're some other people. Never mind them now.'

Drake nodded. 'Oh, yes? Evening,' he called out.

The centurion stared back without comment.

'Hmm.' Drake turned back to Meg. 'I imagine Art's involved too,' he said. 'So where are these counterfeiters?'

'They have a secret tunnel under the river. You get to it through one of the tombs.'

'You're not having us on, are you?' Drake said suspiciously.

Meg glared at him.

'No,' Drake decided, seeing her expression. 'Of course not. You'd better show me.'

'Art and Flinch are down there,' Meg said as she led Drake and half a dozen uniformed policemen over to the tomb. 'And Mr Worthington from the museum, he went down after them. They should be back by now.'

'They should be in bed by now,' Drake countered. 'So should you and Jonny, come to that.'

'Sir – look!' one of the policemen shouted.

Ahead of them, the lid of the tomb was slowly tilting open. Meg drew in her breath, hoping against hope. But the face that emerged – illuminated fully in the light of a policeman's torch – belonged to no one that Meg knew. It was the weathered, startled face of a middle-aged man. He blinked in the light.

'Hold it!' Drake shouted. 'Police.'

'Strewth!' the man said, and he disappeared.

The lid of the tomb began to slide back into place. Policemen ran to grab it, forcing it open again.

Drake and Meg stood at the top of the staircase concealed inside the tomb. Drake and the police shone their torches down, picking out the brick-lined walls and the stone steps.

'Right, then,' Drake decided, 'we'd better see what's down there. But we'll go carefully.

They may be armed and dangerous.' He turned to Meg. 'I'll leave Hodges up here with you. He's by the gate. And Lord Fotherington will be on his way over, I imagine.' He looked back towards the gate, towards the broken circle of Roman soldiers. 'Yes,' he said quietly, 'well, let's get going, then.'

As the last of the policemen climbed into the tomb and disappeared from sight, Meg turned to go. She might as well wait with PC Hodges at the gate for Charlie and Jonny, she decided. But then a scraping, clanking sound – a heavy, metallic rumble – emerged from the tomb. She turned back quickly, wondering if she should follow Art's dad and the others down to see what was happening.

But after several moments, Art's dad emerged from the tomb, his men behind him. They all looked grim.

'What is it? What's happening?'

'Doors. Huge metal doors. Swung shut before we could get through. Reilly here nearly got crushed.'

'Flood gates,' Meg said. 'Art mentioned them.'

'Well, flood or no flood, they're shut now. And there's no way we're going to get through them.' Drake was looking drawn and pale. 'Art and the others are trapped down there.'

The smog from outside seemed to have crept into the warehouse. What light there was shone through the murky air and the broken windows from the streetlamps outside. Jonny knew his way round so well that he was able to navigate through the sea of broken packing cases, discarded rolls and piles of carpet, treacherously rotted floor-boards . . . He knew the Cannoniers' den as well as he knew his own home.

But there was not enough light to see if the bone was still resting on top of the roll of carpet where he had last seen it, where he had watched Art put it down without ever thinking it would turn out to be so important. He was right up by the carpet before he could be sure of what he had gradually realised as he approached.

The bone was gone.

Jonny looked round, checked beside the carpet in case it had fallen. Art must have moved

226

it, tidied it away. Maybe he had taken it home, who could tell? In a blur of speed, Jonny checked everywhere he could think of. Then he checked again. Still nothing. Had he missed it? Or was the bone simply no longer here? Should he continue searching, or should he give up and get back to Meg at the graveyard? In near despair, he sat down on a length of carpet and put his head wearily in his hands.

Galman had run right past Flinch and Art. He was out of breath as he arrived in Bablock's office, leaving the door wide open behind him. Flinch could see him gasping for breath beside Worthington.

'Police,' he gasped. 'Marsden says there are police in the graveyard.'

Bablock gave a snarl of anger. 'Then close the gates, you fool.'

'Marsden's doing it now,' Galman replied.

As he spoke, there was a distant rumble like metallic thunder.

'We'll never get out now,' Art said quietly.

'We're trapped,' Galman all but whimpered.

'Don't be absurd,' Bablock told him. 'We can

open this end of the tunnel and be gone before the police ever get through.'

'But what if they come through both ends?'

'If they've found one entrance to the tunnel, it's through luck. Or carelessness. But we hardly use the other end, so no one will know where that emerges.'

'You're sure?' Galman sounded relieved. 'Oh, er, you asked for this.'

Flinch saw he was holding a large hammer. He handed it to Bablock.

'You know, I don't think that's a very good idea,' Worthington said. He was edging back towards the door.

But Bablock levelled the gun at him, taking the hammer in the other hand. 'What isn't a good idea?' He was standing behind his desk again, raising the hammer.

'What you're planning to do with that hammer,' Worthington said. 'I wouldn't. I really, *really* wouldn't.'

Galman looked from Worthington to Bablock. 'What does he mean? What shouldn't you do?'

'This,' Bablock said simply.

And smashed the hammer down into the top of the stone casket.

The stone fractured along the line of the crack. Dark smoke seemed to be curling up from it. Bablock was still staring at Worthington, but now it was not just his pupils that were black. The whole of his eyes were like dark stones set in his head. The mist from the casket was thickening, rising, becoming a foggy cloud of blackness.

'Good grief,' Galman gasped. 'What is it?'

Bablock dropped the hammer. He reached across the desk, grabbed Galman's hair and wrenched forwards – pulling the man's head into the dark cloud.

Galman screamed. Bablock howled with inhuman laughter. Worthington took another step backwards.

Then Galman was staggering away, his hands to his face as if he had been burned. He was still screaming, but the sound was changing, was merging with Bablock's laughs. Both men were laughing. And when Galman dropped his hands away from his face, his eyes were like lumps of coal, burning with a dark inner light as he and his master turned towards the door. The black cloud floated, expanded, deepened between them.

Darkening.

There was a storm coming. It was early evening, but already the sky was black. Thunder rumbled ominously in the distance and a light rain was starting to fall.

'This is a really bad idea, you know that?' Sarah said. She hugged her coat tight about her as the rain got heavier. 'Like, *really* bad.'

'You saw his eyes,' Arthur insisted. 'You heard what Grandad said.'

'Hanging round a deserted graveyard, after dark, waiting for a celebrity possessed by an ancient pagan devil.' Sarah shook her head, sending her long dark hair into a whirl. 'Not my idea of fun.'

'Someone's got to do it,' Arthur said. 'Anyway, it isn't dark, not really. And we're hoping he isn't possessed. *You* don't think he is,' he pointed out.

'I don't know what to think.'

They made their way slowly along the path heading towards the mausoleum.

'If Grandad's right, this is where the thing's power will be greatest. And it will need to gather its strength.'

'I don't know how he works that out,' Sarah grumbled.

It was raining quite hard now and the thunder was an almost constant backdrop.

'Because there weren't possessed or dead bodies lying round the Embankment after that news conference, I suppose.'

'True enough,' Sarah admitted. 'But you were wrong about this graveyard.'

'Oh?'

She pointed further along the path. It was difficult to see now, it was so dark and the rain was angling in on them. Arthur blinked it away and could just make out a figure walking towards them. A man. For a moment his head was silhouetted against a pale patch of sky, and Arthur could see that he was wearing what looked like a helmet.

'So you can see him this time,' Arthur realised. 'That man I saw,' he went on, 'he said something about wielding a sword of truth.'

231

'You think he really meant it?'

'Let's ask him.'

The figure stopped on the path several yards in front of them. 'Oh,' it said, 'you again. I thought I told you . . .'

His words were drowned out by a rumble of thunder. At the same moment, the sky was lit by a sheet of sudden lightning.

Sarah laughed. 'You thought he was a Roman soldier, didn't you?' she told Arthur.

The flash of lightning had only lasted a second. But it was long enough for them both to see the policeman clearly. 'Come on, you two,' he said. 'Haven't you got homes to go to?'

'Yes,' Sarah shouted back at him, 'we have.' She took hold of Arthur's arm. 'There's no point in hanging round here.'

It was pouring now and they were both drenched.

'I suppose not,' Arthur admitted. 'I did think Martin Michael might come here.' He shrugged, blinking the cold rain out of his eyes. 'I was wrong. Sorry,' he called to the policeman, 'we're going.'

But the policeman's only reply was a choking retch. His hands were clutching at his throat and he was shaking. His helmet tilted sideways before falling to the ground, thudding on to the gravel path. The policeman looked up at them, his eyes black as night. Then, slowly, the eyes rolled upwards, giving a glimpse of white, before he slumped unconscious to the ground.

Behind him, lit up by the lightning that now crackled round the gravestones and over the tombs, stood Martin Michael. He raised his arms high in the air and the stabs of lightning seemed to flow from his fingers up into the sky.

'Soon.' His voice echoed through the breaking storm. 'The power grows. Soon I shall feed again on the impure and the invaders.'

'OK, Arthur,' Sarah said, her voice shaking. 'So you were right. What now? How do we stop him?'

Arthur had no idea. But before he could admit it, another voice spoke.

'Wield the sword of truth.'

It was a voice heavy with accent, steeped with age and wisdom. Beside them was standing the man who had spoken to Arthur before. Only now, up close, Arthur could see he was wearing armour. Roman armour.

'I must have my sword,' he said again.

Michael was still standing in the eye of the storm, lashed by the rain and illuminated by the lightning. He was looking straight at Arthur and Sarah. And he was laughing.

CHAPTER ELEVEN

The black cloud hung in the air between the three men. Bablock, laughing, on the far side of the desk; Galman turned towards the door, eyes black as night; Worthington backing slowly away.

Without thought for himself, Art ran into the room. He could hear Flinch shouting at him to come back, but he ignored her. He grabbed Worthington's arm, dragging him towards the door. In front of them, the dark cloud seemed to gather itself and rear up angrily. Then it dived towards them.

As soon as they were through the door, Flinch slammed it shut. It shuddered in its frame, and wisps of black smoke emerged from the sides, the top, underneath – blotting out all light from the room behind.

'Come on!' Art yelled.

They dragged Worthington between them towards the service tunnel.

'We'll be seen,' Worthington protested.

'We know another way,' Flinch told him.

'And we'll be infected by the Darkening if we

hang around,' Art said. 'You saw what happened to Galman.'

He risked a look back, over his shoulder. Maybe it was his imagination, but the tunnel behind them seemed darker than ever. Then, as he watched, a light not twenty feet away seemed to dull, fade and die. From somewhere within the approaching dark cloud, he fancied he could hear laughter.

They reached the point where the service tunnel broke away from the main concourse. Flinch led the way into the side tunnel and they took cover behind the first of the large pillars.

'He was right,' Worthington said. His face was pale and he was flustered. 'That centurion, he was right about the Darkening. About everything.'

'So it seems,' Art agreed.

'We have to get out of here. Goodness only knows what we do then.'

'We can't get out,' Flinch told them. 'They shut the flood doors. We heard them.'

'Of course, yes,' Worthington realised.

'Can the soldiers get in?' Art asked. 'Did they appear, the rest of them?'

Worthington quickly told them what had

happened. They darted across the open space to the next pillar.

'So we're on our own.' Art had to talk loudly now to be heard above the machinery.

'What can we do?' Flinch wanted to know.

From her tone, Art guessed she thought he had a plan. If only that were the case.

But he had no time to confess the truth. A cry from the main tunnel area made all three of them pause and look out from behind the pillar. A man was standing at the end of the tunnel, pointing.

'What the heck's that, then?' he was shouting.

'Don't get too close,' another man shouted back. 'Could be fumes or anything.'

The first man backed away as a dark cloud, like heavy smoke, rolled towards him from the end of the tunnel.

'I don't like the look of it,' the first man said, shaking his head. He paused, leaning forwards to take a close look.

The Darkening leaped forward – a sudden rolling motion, like a black cat pouncing. An enormous hand of smoke-like blackness smothered the man completely for several moments. Then he staggered back, retching, hands to his throat.

Several other men ran to help. But he was already recovering, turning, grabbing them and pushing them bodily into the Darkening. Even from where he was, on the other side of the tunnel, Art could see that the man's eyes were midnight black.

The men staggered out, their own eyes wreathed with darkness. Behind them, Galman and then Bablock stepped into the tunnel.

Bablock's voice seemed to carry even above the sounds of the machinery. 'We must leave this place. Destroy it when the tainted unbelievers come. But first – first we shall sate the appetite that we have felt these endless, empty years.'

And the Darkening rolled onwards, towards the shouting, running men.

Jonny held the bone like the baton in a relay race as he sprinted across the city. He could feel the wind whipping his short hair into a frenzy, tugging at his clothes as he ran. He had so nearly given up, deciding that Art had taken the thing home with him. But he had eventually found the long, narrow bone inside the pocket of the large coat Art wore when he was pretending to be Brandon Lake. Art must have put it there ready to produce and wave at the next consulting session of the Invisible Detective. Jonny grinned as he ran – maybe the Invisible Detective really had found the bone and saved the day.

Now, as he neared the graveyard, Jonny wondered if he would be in time, if the bone was indeed the last one, and would bring the final Roman soldier back from the dead. And had he done the right thing talking to Charlie?

His fears were allayed as soon as he reached the gate. There were several large, dark police cars parked in the street outside, and a constable was waiting at the gate – together with Meg and Charlie.

Meg looked relieved. She even smiled as Jonny arrived, breathless and gasping. Charlie clapped him on the shoulder.

'Get your breath back, lad,' he said. 'You've done well.'

Meg had seen what he was holding. She recognised it at once. 'The bone from the den. Of course.' She was really smiling now. 'Jonny, you're so clever to remember.'

He smiled back. 'Is Art here?'

Her smile faded.

It was Charlie who answered. 'Art and Flinch are still in the tunnel. With that historian chappie from the museum.'

'And the police?' Had he sent them in time?

'They can't get in,' Meg said. She took the bone from Jonny. 'Let's hope this is it, this is the last one. Let's hope it works.'

'Works?' Charlie frowned. 'What's all this about bones, then, eh? And,' he went on to Meg, 'you've still not explained who these chaps dressed up in costume are and what they're doing here.'

Jonny had his breath back now, more or less. 'Come and see,' he said.

He took Meg's hand and together they walked across the graveyard. The torch of the policeman followed them into the murky, misty gloom. Soon it was joined by the beams from the torches held by the dozen or so other policemen Jonny could see standing round the tomb. The beams of light followed Jonny and Meg to the edge of the circle of soldiers. They went to the space, the gap where there was a soldier missing. Gently, carefully, Meg placed the bone on the ground in the space. It gleamed in the torchlight – brittle, pale and ancient.

Then it seemed to glow. And in the glow, a figure solidified out of the misty air.

'*Alea iacta est*,' the centurion announced. He nodded, the ghost of a smile visible beneath his helmet.

'The die is cast,' Charlie translated quietly. He was standing behind Jonny and Meg, staring at the soldier who had just appeared. 'I do not imagine for one moment that there is a reasonable, rational explanation for this.'

'Course not,' said Jonny.

The three of them stepped aside. The soldiers were forming up in double file. The centurion strode forwards, marching to the front of the short column. He paused in front of Jonny, Meg and Charlie.

'*Abyssus abyssum invocat*,' he said. Then he turned and marched towards the tomb.

His soldiers followed, their armour clanking in the still of the night.

'What did that mean?' Meg asked.

Jonny shrugged. The police were standing aside, looking puzzled and alarmed as the soldiers in unison drew their short swords. The centurion stepped into the tomb and started to descend.

'My Latin may be rather rusty,' Charlie said, leading them quickly to the gaping mouth of the tomb, 'but I would translate it as something like "Hell calls to Hell." What it *means*, who can say?'

From somewhere below Art's father's voice echoed up. 'What on earth!' Then a moment later, 'Good grief!'

The area at the bottom of the steps was lit by several torches. Jonny could see Sergeant Drake's astonished face clearly as he watched the soldiers arrive at the bottom of the steps. The centurion was already gone.

Now his hand-picked troops were following him. Following him to engage an enemy they had first defeated almost two thousand years before.

Following him right through the solid metal gates that barred the end of the tunnel.

The wires bit into Art's fingers as he pulled at them. But then suddenly, as with the others, they broke free – pulling away from the explosive charge attached to the wall.

'How many of them are there?' Worthington asked. He was already ripping the wires from the next charge, further along the service tunnel.

'No idea,' Art told him. 'I just hope we can find them all.'

Flinch was running ahead, spotting the dull grey boxes in the dim light. Fortunately most were close to lights – the wires that led back to the control lever in Bablock's office probably used the same conduits as the lighting cables, Art thought.

As they worked their way along the tunnel, Art tried not to listen to the cries and screams from close behind them. Occasionally he looked into the main tunnel, occasionally he dared to see what was happening. Each time he did, the Darkening seemed bigger and closer. And with it – in front, alongside, shambling as silhouettes within its depths – came the walking dead. Their eyes like black stone, their faces twisted into rictus grins as they stalked after yet more victims.

At first it had been easy for the Darkening. But as the forgers realised what was happening, they turned to run. From the cries and shouts further down the tunnel, Art guessed that now they had found the flood doors were closed. Though hadn't Bablock said they could be opened from the inside? Was there some other reason for the screaming from the end of the tunnel? Had

243

whoever closed the gates locked them or destroyed the opening mechanism?

Worthington was looking drawn and tired as they both reached the next explosive together.

Art was grave. 'The way that cloud is expanding, it will soon fill the whole width of both tunnels.'

'Can we get out?' Flinch asked. 'Can we open the gates at the end?'

'Let's hope so,' Worthington said.

'Yes, Flinch,' Art told her with a confidence he didn't feel. 'I'm sure we can.'

Wisps of blackness were drifting into the tunnel behind them, rolling onwards – closing the distance. Art ripped out the wires and ran on. Looking down the service tunnel, he could see several more of the grey explosive charges attached to the wall. Worthington was hurrying to attack the first, Flinch was bouncing up and down beneath the next – too short to be able to reach it, waiting for help. Beyond that, the tunnel turned back towards the main route. Art wondered if that was booby-trapped too.

Worthington finished with the next charge and turned to hurry on. Art caught him up. They looked down the tunnel towards where Flinch was waiting. Both of them stopped. Flinch frowned, turned to see what they were looking at, then ran to join them.

Men were backing down the tunnel, coming their way. Something was driving them on, away from their only escape from the Darkening.

Beyond the men, illuminated by one of the lights, armour shining eerily, stood a Roman soldier. His sword was drawn and he started slowly down the tunnel, marching purposefully forwards. His feet thumped noisily into the stone floor, and Art realised that it was not just this soldier's feet he could hear, but many. In the main tunnel, he could now see the other soldiers – a dozen in all, following their centurion into battle.

Seeing the black-eyed enemy, they levelled their swords, let out a cry and charged.

The men backing away down the service tunnel shrieked with fear, turned and ran. Right towards the Darkening now spreading across both tunnels. They rushed past Art, Flinch and Worthington. Art tried to grab at them, to tell them they had less to fear from the soldiers than the black cloud. But it was no good.

A final figure loomed out of the main tunnel and stood in front of Art – the centurion. He raised his sword in salute. In the main tunnel, the possessed men rushed to do battle with the soldiers, attacking them with hammers, crowbars, levers – anything they could lay their inhuman hands on. The tunnel rang with the sound of metal striking metal. Added to the noise of the machines, still stamping out coins and notes, it was deafening.

Worthington was speaking to the centurion. They both shouted to be heard. Finally the centurion shook his head, raised his sword once again and turned away. With a cry of determination, he ran to join his men, his sword almost glowing in the dull light of the tunnels.

'What did he say?' Flinch demanded.

'He said they can destroy the men possessed by the Darkening – all except the original host,' Worthington shouted back. 'He said we should get out of here while we can and prepare.'

They were hurrying down the tunnel – away from the fighting, the shouting, the rolling black cloud of the Darkening.

'Prepare for what?' Art shouted back.

'The end of the world.'

Art skidded to a halt. 'What! Can't they stop it?'

Worthington was shaking his head. He pulled out a large grubby handkerchief and wiped his glistening forehead. 'No. It is too much for them now. Over the years the Darkening has grown stronger while their own vitality has been sapped away. The casket is broken and they have no other suitable container – that casket was specially prepared apparently, bound up with spells and ancient magic. So they can't contain it, and the Darkening is too concentrated for them to disperse it. Even his specially charmed sword won't destroy it now.'

'Concentrated?' Flinch said.

'There's no way of weakening it. No way to dilute it down to a safe level.' Worthington shrugged. 'Something like that. It's not the sort of conversation my Latin was built for, I'm afraid.'

Art stared at him. They were standing at the point where the two tunnels joined. Over Worthington's shoulder, Art could see a dull grey metal box on the wall. 'You go on,' he said. 'Get to the way out and open the gates. Wait for me there.'

'What are you going to do?' Flinch asked.

'I'll try to send as many of those men to the way out as I can. Then we must seal the gates again.'

'Trap the Darkening down here?' Worthington said.

'Something like that.'

'Will that work?' Flinch said.

'Let's hope so. Go on.'

'No,' Worthington said firmly, 'you two get out of here. Leave this to me.'

But Art shook his head. 'I doubt I'm strong enough to work the flood gates – you'll *have* to do it.' He didn't wait for a protest, but started to turn away.

'I'll come with you, Art,' Flinch decided.

'No, Flinch. Go with Mr Worthington. He'll need your help. Won't you?' he said pointedly to Worthington.

'What? Oh, er, yes – I'm depending on you.' He took Flinch by the hand, nodded a farewell to Art and pulled Flinch after him.

Art watched them for a moment. Forced himself to smile at Flinch as she looked back over her shoulder. Then he turned and ran back down the service tunnel, hoping that he could get past the Darkening to Bablock's office.

As soon as she got the chance, Flinch slipped her hand from Worthington's grasp and ran back down the tunnel to help Art.

'Flinch – come back!'

'I'm helping Art,' she yelled. 'You go on.'

She paused just long enough to be sure that Mr Worthington was about to open the flood doors like Art wanted. Then she ran back down the tunnel after Art. Soon she spotted him in the distance ahead of her. She could see him cautiously approaching the black cloud. He had passed several men, shouted at several more. Some of them had listened – had turned and run back down the tunnel, away from the fighting. Worthington would get them out of the tunnels to safety.

The black cloud seemed to be getting thicker, deeper, wider. It almost reached the outside wall of the service tunnel now. Art squeezed past and Flinch lost sight of him. In the main tunnel, six of the soldiers were hacking at the cloud with their swords. They gouged great slices of blackness from it. But as soon as the dark sections fell away, the main cloud rolled forwards, reabsorbing them. Slowly but inexorably, the soldiers were being driven back down the tunnel as the cloud grew . . .

Flinch took a deep breath and ran. She dived past the billowing blackness, feeling the sudden tug of cold as she slid past. She bounced off the tunnel wall, grazing her shoulder. But she was through.

She looked back and saw that the tunnel was all but filled with the cloud now. As she hesitated, a great fist of blackness rushed out at her. Flinch yelped and ran. Ahead of her she could see Art, also running – back into the main tunnel, and then onwards, into darkness. He was making for Bablock's office.

'I was expecting Gaius Julius Atreus, not some boy.'

Flinch stopped outside the door. The lights inside seemed dimmer now – turned down low. She looked inside.

Bablock was standing in front of his desk. His eyes were black, his face seemed to have darkened – light seemed to be falling into his body. He was holding a gun, and it was pointing at Art, who stood just inside the door.

'What are you doing here?' Bablock demanded. 'You may as well tell me before I kill you.'

'I've come to stop it,' Art said. His voice was quiet but determined. 'To stop the Darkening.'

'*Nothing* can stop the Darkening,' Bablock announced. 'Least of all you.' He levelled the gun.

Flinch did not stop to think. She dived through the door, past Art. She saw Bablock's black eyes widen in surprise, saw the gun begin to move towards her. She hurled herself forwards, head down, smacking into Bablock and sending him reeling.

The gun went off, the shot ricocheting off the ceiling and hammering into the portrait on the wall – tearing out one of the painted eyes so that only a ragged black hole remained. Bablock was sprawled back across the desk, the gun knocked from his hand. Art was looking at Flinch with a mixture of admiration and sadness as she picked herself up from the floor.

'You have got a plan, haven't you, Art?'

'Yes,' he admitted. 'I have.'

He even sounded sad. As he turned slightly, she could almost swear there was a tear on his cheek.

Then, as Bablock struggled to pull himself up, as he scrabbled to retrieve the gun, Art ran across the room, towards the portrait. Towards the control boxes.

'I'm sorry, Flinch,' Art said, and suddenly she knew what he was going to do.

His hand slammed down on the lever of the right-hand box. From somewhere in the distance, above the screams and shouts and the sounds of battle, came the low percussive roar of the charges as they exploded into the fabric of the tunnel and ripped through the roof.

Arthur and Sarah ran, feet splashing through the puddles, driving rain soaking them to the skin. Away from the graveyard the storm seemed less intense, but it was still fierce. They were running into the wind, struggling to make headway.

'How long?' Sarah gasped.

'How long will it take?' Arthur managed to reply.

She shook her head, showering him with more water. 'How long have we got?'

He had no idea. 'Just keep running.'

They saw no one. The storm had cleared people off the streets. Arthur had half hoped to flag down a taxi. But there weren't even any cars or buses. They were hardly in the heart of the city, after all, and the water was running off the streets as if they were shallow rivers.

At last they reached Myton Gardens. The dark shape of the museum loomed out of the gathering night and the blackness of the storm. They all but collapsed gratefully in the doorway.

'How do we get in?' Sarah wondered. 'Break a window or what?'

Without any idea, Arthur reached for the handle of the door.

It turned before he touched it. The door opened and Miss Worthington stood there, looking at them in disbelief. 'Well,' she said. 'I wasn't expecting you again. You'd better come in.'

'You're still open?' Arthur asked in disbelief as they stood dripping inside the doorway. Before long they were both standing in puddles.

'Of course we're not open.'

'Then why—' Sarah began.

'I was waiting,' she said. 'My father told me that one day there would be someone.'

'Your father?' Arthur said. 'You mean Mr Worthington?'

She nodded. 'When I saw that man's dreadful eyes on the television, I knew it was time. Just as he said. Just as he warned me, all those years ago. Though I don't think even he believed it would ever happen. Not again.' She looked from Arthur to Sarah. 'But it has, hasn't it?'

'Yes,' Sarah said. 'I didn't want to believe it either, but it has.'

'Of course, I was expecting a Roman gentleman.' She led them further into the museum. 'Bit disappointed not to be able to try out my Latin, actually. But then, you can't have everything, can you?' She stopped beside the display case housing the sword and the stone casket. She lifted the transparent cover from the table and put it on the floor. 'This is what you came for?'

Arthur nodded. 'He speaks English now. A bit, anyway.'

'Seems we have all been preparing.' She gestured to the sword. 'Well, best not waste any more time.' She sniffed. 'I didn't catch your names.' It sounded like an accusation.

The sword would be heavy, very heavy with the stone casket attached to it, Arthur realised. He hoped the centurion would be able to smash it off the blade or something. He wouldn't worry about damaging an ancient relic after all. Arthur took hold of the handle of the sword.

'I'm Sarah and this is Arthur.'

He tugged at the sword. It seemed to tingle in his grasp, as if charged with electricity. Then, without any apparent difficulty, it pulled easily from the stone, as if he was merely drawing it from its sheath.

'Arthur, eh?' Miss Worthington said. 'Well, that seems appropriate. Now, you must hurry.'

'Aren't you coming with us?' Arthur called back to her as they ran for the door.

'I'd only slow you down. You go – now!'

Outside it seemed darker than ever. Lightning played across the sky, arcing down towards a point in the distance – the graveyard at Northerton. Arthur lifted the sword, testing its weight. Watching its pale glow in the darkness.

CHAPTER TWELVE

They wouldn't let Jonny or Meg into the tunnel. Even when the heavy metal doors finally swung open to reveal Mr Worthington standing on the other side, Charlie held them back.

The police took charge of the men who emerged – frightened and confused. They handcuffed them and led them up the stone steps to the graveyard. Sergeant Drake stayed at the bottom of the steps with Worthington and Charlie. Waiting, with Jonny and Meg, for Art and Flinch.

'Flinch was with me,' Worthington said sadly. 'She went back to help Art.'

'Help him do what?'

Worthington shook his head. 'Get people out, I suppose. That's what he said.'

Drake was organising the police who remained at the entrance. 'That's enough hanging around twiddling our thumbs,' he decided. 'Whatever is really happening in there, we're going to find out.'

'I really wouldn't advise it, sir,' Worthington said.

But Drake shook off his protests. 'There are

still people in there. If there is danger, as you suggest, then that's even more of a reason why we need to go in and help. If nothing else, we must stop Bablock and the other ringleaders escaping from the other end of the tunnel.'

Worthington gave a heavy sigh and stepped aside.

'We're coming with you,' Meg announced.

'Yes,' Jonny agreed, though he dreaded what they might find.

Drake opened his mouth. Jonny was certain he was about to tell them to stay put. Charlie put his hand on Jonny's shoulder.

Then the ground shook and dust showered down from the roof. A burst of successive huge explosions roared through the open flood doors.

'Oh, my giddy aunt,' Worthington said in the hush that followed. 'He's set off the explosives.'

'What explosives?' Drake demanded.

The dust was a fine mist in the air around them, swirling in the torchlight.

'Bablock had the tunnels mined. To flood them and destroy the evidence if he was discovered.'

There was another sound now. A growing

rumble. Somewhere along the tunnel Jonny was sure he could hear water dripping.

'We can't go in there now,' Drake said, his voice hoarse with emotion. 'The whole place may collapse at any moment.'

It was unmistakably the sound of dripping water. The drips became heavier, like a tap slowly being turned on.

'We'd better close the flood doors,' Worthington said. 'The controls are just through here.' He took a step back towards the tunnel mouth.

Drake grabbed his shoulder and dragged him back, turning him round. 'You can't,' he yelled. 'There are still people down there.'

The sound of the water was louder now. A narrow, dark stain was spreading down the tunnel towards them. Water started to drip from the ceiling close by – soon becoming a fine spray, then a shower.

Charlie pulled Drake's hand away from Worthington. 'The land here is lower than the level of the river,' he said, his voice measured and calm. 'We may *have* to close the flood doors.'

'We can't,' Drake said again, his voice barely

a whisper now, his whole body shaking. 'What about Art?'

Jonny swallowed. He looked at the water, now pouring through the roof and splashing along the tunnel. In minutes – maybe only seconds – it would be completely flooded. 'I'll get him,' he said, and ran.

Behind him, Meg made to follow. But Charlie caught her arm and pulled her back.

'We can't lose you too,' he said, and his eyes were as wet as the tunnel floor.

As soon as he hit the lever, Art turned, grabbed the casket and dragged Flinch to her feet.

'Come on!'

Bablock was close behind them as they dashed from the room and out into the darkened tunnel.

'What's that for?' Flinch shouted.

Art realised she meant the casket. 'Don't want it taking refuge inside,' he gasped. 'We need to dilute the Darkening – the power of water, remember, like the centurion said. Now run!' He hugged the casket to his chest.

This part of the tunnel at least was intact. But

would the roof have collapsed at the exit? They could not head for the other end of the tunnel – Bablock was in the way. In any case, Art had no idea how far it might be before the tunnel surfaced. If it ever did.

They slowed as they approached the black cloud that filled the tunnel. It seemed to be boiling in anger. The smoke-like Darkening fizzed and popped. A shape loomed up out of it – hand raised as if to strike at them.

And the centurion stepped from the smoky air. He was hacking at the Darkening for all he was worth, tearing great chunks out of it with his sword. Behind him, more of the soldiers were just visible – smudged outlines within the cloud. The centurion paused as he saw Art and Flinch. He raised his sword, and Art saw that it was glowing with a pale inner light.

Then the centurion turned and shouted an order to his men inside the Darkening. In moments, a tunnel started to appear. To either side of this narrow tunnel through the cloud the Roman legionaries hacked and cut and struck with their swords. Carving a safe passage through the middle of the Darkening.

Art glanced back and saw that Bablock was running towards them. A shot whined into the heavy air, cracking off the breastplate of one of the soldiers.

Art grabbed Flinch's hand and dragged her through the black cloud. On both sides of them the soldiers worked furiously to keep the Darkening back. Even so, Art could feel the clammy fingers tearing at him as they ran. Then, suddenly, they were through and out the other side.

Straight into a crowd of black-eyed men who gave a collective roar of rage and rushed at them. A hammer slammed through the air towards Art's head. He braced himself for the blow, knowing it would shatter his skull.

But instead it clanged heavily into a sword. One of the soldiers stepped from the blackness and thrust the hammer away, following up with a swift stab that sent the man staggering backwards with a cry.

Art didn't wait to see what happened. He and Flinch were running again, splashing through the tunnel, water pooling at their feet. A wave was coming up the tunnel towards them, and now they could hear the crash and thunder of the Thames breaking through the weakened roof.

Spray blinded them. Somewhere close by, a light exploded as the water got to the bulb. Then another. The tunnel was plunging into darkness. Art fumbled for his torch. The beam illuminated a showering cascade – a waterfall from the breaking roof. Bricks and chunks of cement were crashing down with the white foaming torrent. Together Art and Flinch staggered into the water, on and through and out the other side. On to the next break in the roof.

Dark lines cracked across the brickwork of the ceiling, linking up, water tearing through. It was impossible to see where they were going, which direction the tunnel led. They might turn and head back into the Darkening without ever knowing.

Except for the shouts from up ahead. Jonny's frantic cries: 'Art! Flinch! Where are you?' Something to head for.

And then the flood doors – closing. Jonny grabbing Art's hand.

'They're closing the doors,' Art gasped, his throat full of water.

'No, your dad won't let them. It's the pressure of the water, forcing them to close.'

Whatever the reason, the doors were swinging slowly shut. The heavy metal was closing in, cutting off their escape. They had to jump as much as run to wade quickly through the rising water, to get to the doors. And only when they reached them, only when Art had thrust Jonny through the closing gap, only as he prepared to squeeze through after his friend . . . only then did Art realise that Flinch was no longer holding his hand.

Water rose and bubbled and boiled around him. The gap between the doors in front of him narrowed. Still there was no sign of Flinch.

Jonny's arm emerged from the other side of the doors and dragged Art towards them. 'Come on, Art!'

'I can't!' he protested. 'Where's Flinch?'

But his shouts were lost in the thunder of the water. He was off balance, slipping, falling, dragged through the doors before they closed. Vaguely aware of the figures standing above the water on the steps. His father diving down into the rising tide and reaching out for him.

Then a hand, small and pale, clutching through the doors after him. Flinch.

Art grabbed the hand and pulled. 'Help me!' he yelled.

Jonny was at his side, reaching for the hand.

Flinch's face emerged above the water, choking and spluttering, but still on the wrong side of the closing doors. And behind her another face. Bablock – his eyes blazing like burning coals, his arms reaching round Flinch to drag her back.

Art felt his grip failing. Flinch's hand was torn from his own. Bablock's arms laced round her neck, dragging her down into the foam. For a second her long fair hair floated on the surface. Then it too was gone.

The doors clanged shut, cutting off the sounds of the flood. Leaving them alone, waist-deep in water under the graveyard.

Jonny's face was white. His dark hair was plastered across his head, his mouth open. 'Flinch?' he murmured.

As he spoke, the water between Jonny and Art erupted like a geyser. A torrent sprayed upwards as wet hair flew and twisted, showering

Art and Jonny with a blizzard of droplets. In the middle of it Flinch choked and struggled for breath.

'Worse than a bath!' she gasped.

Arthur was running like the wind now. Sarah had shouted at him to go ahead, to get back to the graveyard as fast as he could. She was falling behind as he ran, the sword glowing in his hand. He could imagine Jonny making this same journey – running even faster through and towards the darkness, carrying a bone the size of a sword and every bit as potent as a weapon.

The man was waiting for him. He looked old and tired but relieved when he saw Arthur arrive. In the centre of the graveyard, Michael was standing exactly as he had been when Arthur left. Except that now he was surrounded by a halo of blackness, as if the night itself was congealing around him.

'Here,' Arthur said, breathless and ready to drop from exhaustion. He held the sword out to the man in armour. 'Take it.'

But the man made no effort to reach for it. 'It is not for me,' he replied. 'I too need to gather my strength.' He held out his arm, turning to indicate the area behind him – the faint figures that were just discernible through the gloom. Yet another flash of lightning showed the ethereal outlines of the soldiers standing to attention in the shadows. 'Soon,' the man said. 'But not yet.'

'It'll be too late!' Arthur yelled at him. 'Look!' He pointed at Michael, the blackness spreading round him, his laughter echoing round the cemetery.

'I am sorry.' He did reach for the sword now. Reached out to take it, and let Arthur see how his hand passed through the handle of the sword.

Arthur looked into the man's sad face, realising that he could see through it to where Michael was standing beyond. 'What must I do?' he asked, his voice barely a whisper.

'Use the sword. Save us all.'

'I don't know how!' Arthur yelled, panic gripping him.

The centurion stepped aside, gesturing for Arthur to advance on the gathering blackness. 'Let the sword guide your hand,' he said. 'It knows what to do.'

With a mixture of apprehension and disbelief, Arthur walked slowly towards Michael. The laughter had stopped now. The lightning had stopped. The man's dead black eyes watched him all the way across the graveyard. The Romans were probably watching him too, but Arthur did not look to see. All his attention was focused on Michael, on the Darkening around him ... On the way the blackness was moving, shifting, coalescing in Michael's outstretched hand.

A sword of black night was forming. Michael was advancing on Arthur, spinning the dark sword like the expert he was. Any moment, it would come shattering down.

Arthur raised his own sword, now glowing brightly, ready to try to parry the performer's blow, hoping against hope ...

The swords met – light and dark. A metallic crash in the graveyard. Arthur's hand seemed to be working without him, without any effort or thought. The sword was doing the work, dragging him along as it thrust and cut and blocked.

Again and again Michael struck at Arthur. Again and again Arthur's sword blocked the blow. Each time, the sword glowed a little brighter, Michael's black sword became a little fainter. Like light shining into shadows and dispelling the darkness.

The sword was pulling his hands in the right direction, guiding his movements. But with each and every blow, Arthur could feel his strength seeping away. He thrust forward desperately, and their arms locked as the swords met like two intertwined snakes. Michael's eyes seem to glow with blackness as he bore down on Arthur, forcing him to the cold, wet ground. The swords parted, met again. Arthur tried desperately to block the next blow, letting the sword pull him. His whole arm was jarred by the impact. He was lying on his back now, in the mud. A gravestone above his head. The sword was knocked from his grip and flew through the air. It thudded into the ground several feet away – out of reach.

Michael stepped forward, feet on either side of Arthur's prone body, sword raised in triumph. Then scything down, towards his head. Blackness rushing in. Arthur unable to close his eyes or look away as the blade hammered towards him.

And crashed into the glowing blade of his own sword as it was thrust across.

Michael went reeling back in surprise, and the centurion followed – thrusting and cutting with the glowing sword, driving the Darkening that had been Martin Michael towards the semicircle of legionaries stepping from the shadows. The Romans drew their swords. Arthur looked away. Michael's screams rang through the graveyard as the rain stopped, the clouds drifted away and the first pale shards of moonlight shone down on the muddy ground.

A hand helped Arthur to his feet. He realised that it was Sarah. Miss Worthington was standing beside her.

'You all right?' Sarah asked.

It was all Arthur could do to nod.

The soldiers were still standing in their semicircle. But as Arthur watched, they faded slowly away. All but one. The centurion, striding towards Arthur. He looked younger, stronger. He was smiling. He raised the sword, holding it by the glowing blade so the handle made the sign of the cross over his face.

'*Tu fui, ego eris*,' he said. Then slowly he faded away. The glow from the sword lingered a moment, than that too was gone.

'You got some Latin after all,' Arthur said. He was surprised how weak his voice sounded.

'If you're sure you're all right,' Sarah told him, 'I'll see to Michael.'

He hadn't realised that Michael was still there, lying on the ground, in a puddle of moonlight. 'Be careful,' Arthur said, watching her run to him.

Miss Worthington took his arm and led him slowly after Sarah. 'Literally translated, it means, "I was you, you will be me." You see it on gravestones.' She looked round. 'Appropriately enough.'

Michael was sitting up, taking in his surroundings with evident confusion. Arthur gently shook off Miss Worthington's arm and crouched down beside Sarah. He stared into Michael's eyes – and saw that they were normal. Scared and bewildered, but normal.

'I think he's OK,' Sarah said. She reached out to help him.

'What you doing, you daft girl?' Michael said, pulling back.

Sarah reached out again. 'I'm trying to help you.'

'Don't touch me,' he protested. 'No one touches me. Not without permission. I'm famous, I am. A star. Get your grubby hands off, you hear me?'

Sarah stood up. 'Yes,' she said quietly, 'I hear you.'

Arthur stood up too and took her hand. 'Sorry,' he murmured. Then he turned to Miss Worthington. 'Has it gone?' he asked. 'Is it finished?'

'Who can tell?' she said. 'But I think, yes. I think it is over. The Darkening was weakened by the water of the Thames. This really was its last hope, its last chance. And now . . .'

'Yes?' Sarah prompted her, sparing Michael a quick glance.

'Well, now I think we could all do with a cup of tea,' Miss Worthington announced.

Michael was struggling to his feet. 'Oi,' he said, 'where are we? What am I doing here? Where's my limo?' He stared accusingly at Sarah. 'I'm supposed to be at the Ritz this evenin.'

'Find your own way there,' she told him.

CHAPTER THIRTEEN

Most of the cars had left, taking the police and their captives with them. Curious locals had been shepherded away and the graveyard was once again quiet. But it was not deserted. A small group of people were gathered outside the mausoleum. In front of them, thirteen Roman soldiers stood in a circle.

'I'll leave a policeman on duty here until you remove the coins and relics,' Sergeant Drake told Mr Worthington.

'I'm sure Sir Henry will give you a hand cataloguing it all,' Charlie said.

'That would be kind,' Worthington said gratefully. 'I intend to open a special section at the museum. Just a few relics, I think. The rest I shall return to their proper resting place here. Along with the bodies of the brave soldiers who died all those years ago.' He looked across at the shadowy figures standing watching.

Art and Jonny and Flinch were wrapped in blankets. Meg was almost as wet as they were from hugging Flinch and – after the briefest hesitation – Art and Jonny too. They stood shivering as they listened.

'Time to get you home and into a warm bed,' Art's father told them.

'Miss Flinch had better come home with me,' Charlie said. 'She looks as if she could do with a warm bath, which I'm sure my housekeeper can arrange.' His eyes twinkled with amusement as Flinch bristled at the suggestion of a bath.

'Do you think we did it?' Art asked quickly. 'Is it gone – the Darkening, I mean?'

Worthington nodded. 'So our friend Centurion Gaius believes. He says that it will take it years to regain any sort of strength, if it ever does. And he and his men will be waiting for it. QED.'

'What's that mean?' Flinch asked.

'It's short for *quod erat demonstrandum*,' Worthington told her. 'Latin again. It means "as has been shown".'

Art's dad sighed. 'You learn something new every day,' he said. 'Though it's not a phrase I think I'll need that often myself.'

'The important thing is that the Darkening is gone, at least for now,' Worthington concluded.

In front of them, the centurion seemed for

once to understand what was being said. He nodded, and thumped his clenched fist into his breastplate then out in a brisk salute. The other soldiers followed his example. They stood, fists clenched across their armour, as their leader marched across to the mausoleum. The centurion drew his sword. It was still glowing.

He didn't know why – it just felt right – but Art took out the casket he had still been hugging inside his sodden jacket. He bent down and placed it on the ground at his feet. The top was cracked, one side gashed open. The interior was dark and empty. He stepped away as the centurion raised his sword.

The sword swung down, slicing into the cracked stone. It bit deep into the casket. The centurion let go of the sword and stepped away. He looked at Art and for a moment their eyes locked together. Then the soldier saluted again and faded into the night.

Across the graveyard, the other soldiers were also fading into shadow.

'The Invisible Detective meets the Invisible Soldiers,' Jonny said.

'Don't be silly,' Meg told him.

Flinch giggled and Art smiled.

'The Invisible Detective put us on to the forgers,' he told his dad.

Worthington was examining the casket. He pulled experimentally at the sword, but was unable to move it.

'I'm not even going to ask,' Art's father said. 'I don't know – forgers in underground tunnels under the Thames, people dressed up as Roman soldiers . . .' He shook his head.

Jonny looked about to protest, but Art put a hand on his arm, and Charlie was shaking his head. If that was what Art's dad wanted to think, then let him.

'And where the Invisible Detective is concerned,' Dad was saying, 'I've found it's often better not to know the whole truth.' He smiled. 'QED,' he added.

Martin Michael's apparent mental lapse and memory problems following his underwater ordeal made a late item on the television news.

'Sarah doesn't seem so taken with him now,' Arthur told Grandad. 'Though they're saying his DVD sales have rocketed and he's got a new series coming up on one of the satellite channels.'

'He won't go mucking about in the Thames again in a hurry,' Grandad said.

'That's true.'

'The end of the adventure for him at least.'

'For me too,' Arthur said sadly. 'And it has been an adventure.'

'What do you mean?' Grandad asked.

Arthur turned off the television. 'It was like really being there, reading through the adventures of the Invisible Detective — only being able to find out about them a bit at a time. When I was sort of supposed to or whatever. Talking to Art, to you, by using that special clock.'

'You think it stops now?' Grandad was smiling. The light caught his eyes, making them shine.

'The clock doesn't work any more,' Arthur admitted. 'I tried it last night. After everything, I went to the house on Jursall Street and . . .' He sighed. 'And nothing.'

'You think the adventure has come to an end.' Grandad was nodding, as if he understood. 'You

277

think this is it, and now you'll never know what happened next.'

'Like the end of a book,' Arthur said. 'That was the last adventure in the casebook. Maybe, when I've read them all, it stops. For me, I mean – the clock and everything. I know that you and Jonny and Meg and Flinch went on. But the war was coming, you were growing up.'

Grandad nodded. 'So it was,' he said. 'And so we were. You know, Jonny never mentioned being bullied again after that, so far as I remember.'

'Was that it for the Cannoniers too?' Arthur wondered. 'Was that the last adventure?'

Grandad hauled himself out of his chair. He went over to the desk at the side of the room. Arthur knew he kept some old photographs and other mementoes in the drawers there. It must be so hard, having to part with everything you've lived with all your life, he thought.

'Let me show you something.' Grandad was reaching inside the drawer, rummaging around under his old shoebox of photographs.

'Another picture?' Arthur remembered the thrill of seeing a photograph of the Cannoniers for the first time – standing in the Crystal Palace park.

But Grandad was holding out a book. The binding was cracked leather and there was a hint of gold lettering on the front, though it had long since faded to the point where it could not be read. It was a book that Arthur recognised at once.

'The casebook of the Invisible Detective,' he said out loud. 'But I left it at home. How did it get here?'

'It didn't. At least, not in the way you think.' Grandad handed it to him. He looked as if he was trying not to laugh. 'The casebook of the Invisible Detective,' he repeated. 'Only this –' he tapped the cover – 'is volume two.'